THIS WAS A BAD IDEA

Book One of the Time Keeper's Saga

Cory and Zachary Barber

WORMHOLE BROS.

ISBN: eBook: 979-8-9991013-2-7   Paperback: 979-8-9991013-3-4

Cover design by 100Covers

Wormhole Bros. | wormholebros.com

This is a work of fiction. Names, characters, places, and events are products of the authors' imagination or are used fictitiously.

Printed in the United States of America

First Edition

For all those who said, "Do it!"

contents

Note from the Authors   VI

1. The Apprentice   1

2. The Search   9

3. Ad Praesens (The Present)   18

4. Jopulous   30

5. Fire and Pain   37

6. The Council of the Valkyrie   58

7. The Secret   66

8. The Great Battle   76

9. The Grieving   85

10. The Return   91

To learn more: 103

NOTE FROM THE AUTHORS

MY BROTHER, ZACH AND I started *The Grieving* (as it was originally called) in the Spring of 2016. At the time, it was a fun creativity challenge that absorbed our minds for a couple hours at a time. We never thought for a moment that it would end up published—much less good.

We would make the couple hour drive to our dad's house at least once a month. At some point at our dad's house, I would pull out my laptop and pass it to Zach. He would read my previous addition and proceed to write his own. Neither of us took it too seriously. We just wanted to have fun and see what happened. We refused to give each other any details about our own intent or the direction that we wanted to take it next.

Eventually, a real story started twisting together. So, we kept writing, and in turn, kept liking it more. It was never something that we had thought about sharing with anyone outside of friends and family. But after lots of (probably too) positive reviews from family and friends, we decided that it would be worth sharing. So...here it is!

This particular version has been polished a bit more than the previous rendition that was formally exclusive to Amazon. In addition, we decided to scrap the title *The Grieving*, and go with something that better captures the theme and plot. We hope you enjoy reading it as much as we enjoyed writing it!

Note: ___**C**___ or ___**Z**____ denotes an author change.

THe
APPRenTICe

___C___ I HAVE BEEN time-traveling in secret for two years now. So far, I've only been able to visit one specific place and time.

April 14th, 1865.

My temporal journey always takes me to Ford's theater, where I sit for a few hours before watching John Wilkes Booth assassinate President Abraham Lincoln. I appear suddenly—and conveniently—in a dull-colored dressing room, where I change into more era-appropriate clothes. From there, I make my way to the seats of the theater, where a crowd has gathered to witness *Our American Cousin*, an acclaimed performance by Tom Taylor.

Before the start of the show, Honest Abe himself arrives in the private box above the stage with his wife, Mary. Next to the couple always sits a young Army officer, Henry Rathbone, along with his fiancée, Clara Harris, and the daughter of New York Senator Ira Harris.

I have watched the president take a bullet to the head fifteen times now.

After the first few times, I wondered whether I should intervene, but was always shut down by the thought of altering the future in a terrible way. The Butterfly Effect is a dizzying theory that I'm hesitant to gamble with.

In all fifteen of my travels, I have merely observed and tried my best to minimize my interactions. I invented a device I call the Granradurhatinator. It allows me to travel back to what I now consider the present by shorting out the mechanism with a titanium filament.

In this way, I can send myself back to the moment before I traveled as if it never happened, thereby erasing from existence any drastic changes that I would have inevitably caused to the future. Unfortunately, it is only a one-time use, unless I can find another incredibly rare radurarium core to construct another granradurhatinator. Therefore, I must make every effort count and minimize the impact on the past as much as possible.

___Z___ Gary Barnige has been my butler for six years. He has frequently observed me as I crafted my greatest inventions, but not *this* one.

Every evening when he heads to his quarters, I retreat to my secret laboratory to modify, polish, and perfect Tempus Viator, my time machine.

Today, everything changed. As Gary was dusting my living room bookshelf, he happened to activate the lever to my secret lair. I have always told him, "If you ever find anything odd in my house, come to me immediately." But the ominous glow coming from my precious machine was too tempting for him. From across the house, I heard him walk down the creaky stairs. I jumped up from my desk and rushed down to see what was going on, and...there he was, mouth wide open in astonishment.

He saw it. My creation!

With an audible pinch of worry in his voice, Gary asked me, "Sir...wh...wha...what is this thing?"

I tried to make up a quick lie in my head, but I am no good under pressure, so the truth spilled out. "Gary...this, my friend, is Tempus Viator. A time machine that I have been developing all of my adult life."

"A *time machine?!*" Gary exclaimed. "That's impossible! You can't possibly have a bloody time machine!"

___C___ So, now that the cat was out of the bag, Gary was in, whether he liked it or not. After making him sign a few non-disclosure agreements, I began the lengthy process of explaining my years of work and recent travel experiences.

"I'm hearing what you're saying, but my mind can't comprehend it," Gary stated.
"Don't worry," I assured him. "It will all make sense soon enough."

I spent the next few weeks getting Gary up to speed on everything and emphasizing the importance of not disturbing the past enough to worsen the future. Gary was motivated. He studied the notes that I had taken over the years until he had practically memorized every detail.

Three months later, Gary and I were having breakfast at Grudela's B & B when he broke the silence looming over the table. "I'm ready!"
"You're not ready!" I corrected. "You *think* you're ready, but you still have *much* more to learn."
Gary's face began to turn a dark shade of red. "So, let me get this straight. You invent this time machine and you travel for the first time without knowing *anything* about what to do or what you would encounter, and you *still* think that *I'm* not ready? I've spent the last *seven* months memorizing your notes! I can tell you the exact temperature of the reverse osmosis capacitor at *any* position of the sun in the sky. I can literally quote the exact boot sequence of the..."
"*Alright!* Alright, already," I interrupted. "Point taken. You can travel. However, you *cannot* forget the consequences of making a single wrong move. Talk to the wrong person and you could alter the entire future! We only have one granradurhatinator, Gary! I'm all out of raduranium cores, so

3

construction of another at this moment isn't possible. We cannot risk using it so soon in our research."

Gary sighed, taking in everything that I was saying. "I understand. Believe me. I'm terrified, but at the same time, I've never been more excited in my entire life!"

A feeling swelled in my chest—one I hadn't experienced in a long time: impulsivity.

"Well, it's settled then," I announced. "Courageous men do things even when they don't feel like they're ready, right? Finish your eggs, Gary. Time travel on an empty stomach is not recommended."

___Z___ There we were: two middle-aged men with no clue what the future held—or the past—or even what any of those words really meant. But it was time. Gary was as ready as he could possibly be, and I was anxious to get back to traveling. I told him to meet me in my office at 8 pm that night for a pre-travel briefing.

At 8:13 pm, I finally heard the door creak open. Gary was late and flustered.

"Are you okay?" I asked.

Gary wiped the sweat from his bald head. "I'm a nervous wreck, sir. What if I mess something up?"

"Gary, you *will* mess *everything* up if you don't calm down. It will all be okay. Just remember all that you have learned," I assured.

After a few moments of silence, Gary looked at me and uttered one simple word. "Okaysirithinkimready."

Obviously, he was still flustered! I handed him what was left of a bottle of brandy, which he proceeded to drain over the next five minutes. It didn't take long for him to calm down afterwards.

With a boost of confidence, he slammed his fist on my desk and gave me a long speech regarding his plan for the night. The entire conversation took almost an hour, but it was fascinating.

In short, Gary planned to try to prevent Lincoln's assassination by causing some sort of distraction, although the nature of the distraction had not been discussed.

"Okay, Gary, we are on the same page in that regard," I said. "But first, we need to see how your blood cells react to the reverse oxidation that happens during time travel. And, we need to ensure that you still have full body function and mental awareness when we reach the other side."

Gary looked at me with a smile on his face. "What are we waiting on, sir?"

___C___ I prepared a special temporal suit for Gary that was a duplicate of the one that I travel in. These suits would degrade naturally during the time-travel process, but they were necessary to prevent a type of chemical burn that would otherwise be sustained during entry into the past. I haven't quite figured out the nature of this phenomenon.

Gary's suit did not, however, come with a granradurhatinator to wear underneath. We would need to obtain another raduranium core before I could construct one for his suit. I decided to detach mine from my suit and keep it loose in case I needed to give it to Gary at any point.

I turned on the secondary computer, which would constantly monitor our vitals throughout the trip. Due to space-time constraints, the monitor's results would not be fully available until we returned to the present and synced our suits to the computer. I brewed up a fresh pot of coffee to reinvigorate myself and poured some into a mug to offer to Gary. He surprisingly pushed it away.

"It's just coffee, Gary. It's a pre-travel ritual of mine," I insisted.

"I hate coffee!" Gary exclaimed.

"Do you also hate America, Gary!?" I asked.

"I'm just more of a tea-guy," he said. "You know, sir, coffee isn't an American original..."

I ignored the last comment.

"Well, sorry, but I'm fresh out of tea, so you're just gonna have to drink this or nothing at all."

Gary snorted at that remark.

I instructed Gary to begin the boot sequence on Tempus Viator. I watched over his shoulder as he began the delicate process of starting the machine.

Floppy disk->Compact disk->Internal Hard drive->Universal Serial Bus Flash memory stick->Ghost operating system->

<bootsequenceinitiated>

<fetchingstartupdata>

<applyingusersettings>

<loadingwallpaperofcutetinykittensplayingwithyarn>

<calibratingtimetoggle>

<syncingmailtoserver>

<uploadingbiometricdata>

<systemready>...

"Well done, Gary!" I congratulated.

Even under the heavy influence of the brandy, he still managed to complete the boot process without any discrepancies. I was slightly worried about how the alcohol would affect his body during the travels, but I quickly struck the thought from my mind. I needed to stay focused and not worry so much.

Once the machine was ready, we reviewed my checklist to ensure we weren't forgetting anything.

Boot machine...check.

Suits on...check.

Granradurhatinator turned on...check.

Titanium filament in right breast pocket...check.

Pre-travel urination...nearly forgot...and check!

All systems are a GO.

We made our way over to the pod and squeezed inside. I had recently modified it to (barely) fit two people. Gary was sweating bullets.

"Gary, I know it's easier said than done, but you need to remain as calm as possible," I instructed in a soothing voice.

"Alright, boss. Let me know when to push the button."

"Push it, Gary."

Time and space stole us away. It is a dizzying feeling. I liken the experience to a severe car accident, but on the molecular level.

___Z___The time it takes for us to travel back to 1865 is exactly three and a half seconds, but as your molecules are rapidly taken apart and put back together, your brain interprets a hundredth of a second as a full second. Thus, the trip is perceived to last three hundred and fifty seconds, usually enough time for me to take a quick nap. This time, I used these moments to make sure Gary was still with me and in one piece. I was relieved to see him floating beside me with no signs of chromosomal warping or arterial combustion. There was a slight glow to his pupils, but I brushed off the thought of that being an issue. Gary always did have a sparkle in his eyes.

No sooner had I drifted into a brief doze than I felt gravity pulling my feet back to the ground.

"Wow. That was a bit odd, Gary. Usually, before I wake up from my power nap, I see a flash of blue. This time it was red. Hmm. What color did you see, Gary?"

I squinted in the dim light, but I could only make out a person-like silhouette in front of me. "Did you hear me, Gary?"

A deep, scratchy voice replied, "Pardon me, sir. My name is Franklin Grovtz the Third."

When my eyes adjusted to the light, I got a good look at him—a tall, older man with a blue corduroy suit on.

"Wait, where is Gary?" I asked.

"I don't recall any Gary here tonight, sir, and—may I ask—what sort of outfit are you sporting?" the man questioned.

I looked down at my Slipknot band-tee and blue jeans that were covered in slime from the recently disintegrated suit and immediately screamed, "*GET OUT!*" The man ran out of the room, startled.

I collapsed in a fit of anxiety. The floor was cold and scratchy. I saw an object lying in the corner of the room. It was Gary's watch. I crawled over and grabbed it. The face was shattered, and the hands were spinning rapidly.

Very peculiar, I thought.*What had happened to Gary?*

Based on the presence of his watch, I was sure that he had made it to this dimension.

Mostly.

2

THE SEARCH

___C___ AFTER A FEW minutes of near hyperventilation, I realized that I needed to get my act together and find Gary. I tried to formulate a plan in my head, but the time-travel jet lag was intense this time around, and my head seemed more hazy than usual.

Snap out of it, Jim!

The most immediate action that needed to happen was to change and blend in with this era before I left this room. I unstrapped the granradurhatinator from my chest and set it aside, along with my twenty-first-century clothing. I found appropriate clothing on the dressing rack and put it on. The door was yanked open a moment later. My timing was impeccable. Franklin Grovtz the Third was back, and this time, a Union soldier accompanied him. *POTTER* was inscribed on the man's uniform.

Franklin cleared his throat. "Potter, I found this man moments ago rummaging around in this closet, wearing some inappropriate attire, and when I questioned him, he raised his voice at me. I demand that you make this man apologize for his rude behavior and explain his reason for being in my actors' closet."

The soldier turned his attention from the older man to me. His expression hinted to me that he was waiting for me to explain myself.

"Excuse me, gentlemen," I stated calmly, trying to imitate their accents, "but if you would let me explain, I'm sure I could appease your troubled minds."

Their shoulders seemed to relax after that small statement.

"Now, gentlemen, approximately ten minutes ago, I arrived here on horseback from New Jersey. My clothes were soiled from the ride, so I walked inside to change. Upon entering this lovely establishment, I attempted to locate a dressing room, which I found. I apologize if I have chosen a private room. When you walked in on me moments ago, I was in my skivvies. I was embarrassed and quite caught off guard that you saw me in such a disorderly manner, so I raised my voice at you. I do solemnly apologize for my behavior, but I was merely just trying to change into more appropriate attire before being in the presence of our dear Mr. President."

This long-winded explanation seemed to please the men.

The elderly man spoke, "Alright then, young chap. I apologize for walking in on you, and I accept your apology for your behavior. Now, I do have to tell you that this is indeed a private dressing room, reserved only for my actor, Booth."

I felt my pulse quicken at the mention of the name. "Do you mean John Wilkes Booth, kind sir?"

"Well, yes, of course." Franklin chuckled.

The soldier, who had yet to speak, turned around to leave. "Grovtz, I suspect that I'm no longer needed, so I'll leave you be."

"Thanks very much, Potter. I do apologize for taking your time."

Grovtz turned his attention back to me. "Now then. I trust you will be leaving my dressing room now and attending to the show."

"Of course," I said. "Just let me grab my things."

Franklin nodded and left the room.

I'm standing in the dressing room of the assassin himself, I thought. *Don't get sidetracked. Gary is my priority right now.*

___**Z**___ I looked down at my watch—8:01 pm.

Two hours from now, Lincoln will be assassinated.

10

Or would he? Did my altercation with Grovtz affect the sequence of events for the night?

I had to make sure, so I quietly made my way to an empty row of seats that had a good view of Lincoln's private box.

Minutes later, I was awakened from a light doze by the stage coordinator calling the crowd to attention. The theater was packed, and the show was about to begin. My mind raced as the play dragged on for what seemed like forever.

As the third stanza concluded, I glanced up towards the President. He was sitting in his usual spot with his usual company—9:59 pm. I turned around and closed my eyes, wishing not to see this gruesome murder again.

I'll never unhear the sounds. The crack of the gun. The screech of the screams.

Lincoln was shot. The timeline has remained unaffected so far.

Honestly, I was pretty relieved when Booth careened off the balcony, snapped his leg, and limped off into the crowded street, just as he usually did. The theater was utter chaos; police running around looking for the murderer, medics surrounding the President trying their best to bring back Honest Abe.

Amidst the anarchy, I exited the theater through the side door.

The street on this side of the theater was surprisingly cold and quiet. I needed a place to gather my thoughts and devise a plan to find Gary.

After about twenty minutes of exploring the city, I saw a sign hanging from a cluttered corner shop.

ROOM FOR RENT: $1 PER NIGHT

I walked into the old building, knowing that I had no money that this era would recognize. The place reeked of spoiled cheese and sour wine. The innkeeper was behind the bar, wiping down the drink glasses.

11

As I approached, the man set down the glass in his hand and gave me a stern look.

"Yer not from these parts, are yeh?" he questioned.

"No, sir, I'm not. How'd you figure?"

A chuckle slid through his rotten teeth, "You just look lost, son. That's all."

"I am lost," I agreed, my head pointing towards the floor. "I've no money and my friend is missing. I don't know what to do."

The man paused for a brief moment, then handed me a glass of water and a room key. "Room number two," he said. "The floor creaks and the bed ain't that great, but it's better than ya catchin' cholera out in the streets."

I said to him, "If a man by the name of Gary happens by, would you please send him to my room? He would likely look as lost as I."

"Sure. Now, get up to the room 'fore ma wife sees ya and gives me a fussin'," the kind man instructed.

I thanked him and went up to the room, exhausted.

I was asleep in minutes.

___C___ FIRE... FIRE... *"FIRE, Master Truffle!"*

I opened my eyes to smoke billowing under the door to my room. The bartender for the inn was banging furiously on the door and coughing.

"I'm alright," I shouted. "I'm going out the window."

I collected my thoughts for a moment and frantically searched the room for anything important that I could be leaving behind. I decided that I wasn't leaving anything worth saving and bolted for the window.

Just before I reached it, the floor below it burst into flames. Disoriented, I turned left. Once again, the floor in front of me erupted in flames.

This can't be happening, I thought.

In that moment, I realized I no longer had a clear path out of the flames. Fire surrounded me on all sides. The room was warming up alarmingly fast.

Movement outside the window caught the corner of my eye. A man was standing outside the window and motioning for me to come outside. A wall of flames separated me from the window by at least four feet. The heat on my skin was nearly unbearable now.

I looked back out the window. The man outside looked much closer now. He was most certainly trying to get my attention. I strained to see him through the smoke in the room. I blinked tears from my eyes. That temporarily allowed me to see the figure outside better.

Gary.

Gary is outside!

I ran toward the flames, closer to the window, to see my friend. He was pointing at his watch.

What does that mean?

I tried to yell at him, but only coughed instead. I felt a sharp stinging on the back of my hand and glanced at it. A blister was forming. A bubble grew under my skin, threatening to pop. Pain assaulted my arm as my skin melted before my eyes. My vision blurred until all became dark.

I AWOKE IN A strange bed. It took me several moments to realize where I was and recall the events of the night before. The sunlight was just beginning to pierce the curtains of the inn room. My mind was lagging in a slight dream state.

It was just a dream, Jimmy.

___**Z**___ Seconds later, I heard a loud banging coming from the first floor. I got dressed, grabbed what little possessions I had, and headed downstairs to turn in my room key.

As I walked down the steps, I noticed the inn-keep nailing boards to the windows.

"What's going on, sir?" I asked.

The older man raised his bushy eyebrows at me. "We've run outta money, that's what. Me and the wife are packing up and leavin' town."

I had no interest in small talk at the moment, so I simply handed the man the key, thanked him for his hospitality, and went on my way.

The streets of D.C were bleak. The air was thick with mourning for the late President.

Strolling down 17th Boulevard, my mind started wandering. I thought back to the dream. It seemed so vivid.

As I approached the small town of Alexandria, I noticed an individual walking towards me. Before we crossed paths, I politely moved to the side so we wouldn't run into each other.

Clearly, I didn't move enough. The man's bony shoulder collided with my arm, making me drop my journal. I leaned down to pick it up and saw that the man had dropped something as well.

A watch.

Turning around to gain the gentleman's attention, I saw him begin a full sprint away from me.

My heartbeat accelerated, beads of sweat crept up on my forehead, and a voice in my head whispered, *Run.* ___**C**___ *Follow him!*

I'm not much of a runner, but I was almost certain that after a while we had covered at least a few miles. We had recently run down at least four different alleyways before I finally began to gain on him. The man wasn't speedy, but he was a hair faster than I, and that was all he needed.

It was a battle of will—a war of attrition. I would not give up until my body failed me. My lungs were on fire, and my heart threatened to explode out of my chest, but my legs were just starting to get the hang of it. The man stood no chance.

I wasn't sure exactly why I was chasing him in the first place. But, in my head, I knew I *should* chase him, and I needed to understand why. Maybe catching him would solve the riddle.

Five feet and closing. I could almost reach out and grab the tail of his shirt.

Just a few steps closer.

I half-considered diving to catch his legs, but decided that it was best left to the stunt doubles.

We turned another corner into a long alley. This had to be my chance. I was sure that my lungs would fail after another stretch. I lengthened my stride and reached out as far as I could. My fingers caught a tassel on his shirt. Relief flooded me momentarily, but just before I could solidify my grip on the fabric, I tripped over my own feet.

It was the furthest thing from graceful. The aggression of the fall left me in a slight daze. I lifted my face out of the dirt and listened for footsteps fleeing me, but I heard nothing. I assumed then that I had been briefly knocked out. I looked up into the alley ahead of me. What I beheld was truly astonishing.

The man was there. Standing, but not entirely in contact with the ground. It was as if he had been turned to stone. I looked around to see if I had any other witnesses.

I must be seeing things, I thought to myself.

I approached the man. Sure enough, he was frozen in place. I walked in front of him to get a good look at his face. Time itself seemed to have stopped.

It appeared that before he was rendered motionless, sweat had been flying from his brow, and now those beads were suspended in the air. I was able to catch my breath as I gazed in awe at his facial features. Fear was frozen in his expression. This man was terrified.

But why?

Just as soon as I finished this thought in my head, time seemed to start again, and the man crashed into me like a linebacker with a vengeance.

"*Time Keeper.* Stay away from me!" the man screamed.

"Time Keeper?" I replied. "What are you talking about?"

The man scrambled to his feet and began running again.

"Stay away!" he said again.

I rose to my feet once more to pursue, but a hand seized my arm. I turned and swatted the hand. A friendly but tired face greeted me.

"*Gary!?*" I exclaimed. "Where have you been?! Please, follow me! We have to question that man."

"The filament," Gary said with a solemn look. "Jimmy, do you have the filament?"

"Yes, of course. Why do you ask? What's going on, Gary?" I asked, concerned.

Gary struggled to find words. He was a bundle of emotions.

"Use the filament, sir. Short the granra...device before it's too late. I've spoken to that man. I don't know how, sir, but he knows. He knows everything. He said someone who worked in the theater told him. This is too ridiculous, Jimmy. Please just short the gran-thing before we ruin the future somehow!"

Panic gripped me like a vice. I fumbled through my shirt to find the granradurhatinator. My breathing came to a stop. It was not there.

Frantically, I searched my pockets and patted myself down from head to toe. It was nowhere to be found.

"The dressing room!" I shrieked. "I left the device in the dressing room."

Gary glared at me, and his panic seemed to change to determination. "Well, then we'd better get back to that dressing room and find it before it's too late. It may be too late already."

Trying to evade the terrible thoughts that were screaming in my brain, I ran ahead and led the way back to the theater.

Please, I begged the universe in my mind over and over, *don't let us be too late!*

3

AD Praesens
(THE PRESENT)

Five hours and forty-nine minutes later

___Z___ "Here we are, Gary," I said, gripping my aching knee. "Ford's Theater."

Without saying a word, Gary walked toward the main entrance and pulled on the door handle.

Locked.

The police had shut the theater down for the foreseeable future after the assassination occurred.

His voice full of angst, Gary said, "We have to find another way in, sir."

I motioned for Gary to come toward me and whispered to him, "We shouldn't talk anymore. Someone could hear us."

After nodding in agreement, he began to walk towards the backside of the theater. Gary has always had a tendency to be...a bit loud, so I grabbed him by the arm and signaled him to stand and wait for me to retrieve the granradurhatinator. (Let's call it GranGran from now on, okay, folks?)

Gary understood the plan.

18

I crouched under a mangled fence and made my way to the stage exit in the rear of the building. Not expecting any luck, I twisted and turned the doorknob. To my amazement, it opened. The door creaked as I slowly opened it.

I stepped inside.

Dark and cold, the theater felt exactly as if someone had just been murdered in it. I pressed my hands against the walls, feeling for a candle, lamp, or something to light my way through the vacant rooms. Finally, I came upon what felt like an old oil lamp. I pat down my pocket for the lighter that I have taken everywhere since the days of my smoking habit. I fiddled it out of my pocket and tried to light the lamp.

After a few attempts, I realized that it was out of oil, so I set it down and decided to continue with just the meager flame from the lighter. The inside of the theater looked unrecognizable in the dark. It took me a few moments to figure out where I was—the ticket area.

So Booth's dressing room isn't far away, I thought.

My heart thumped like a marching band as I made my way to the room. The door was open. Trying not to set anything on fire—or burn my thumb with the lighter—, I peeked around the corner and entered the room.

Luck was on my side, after all. GranGran was right where I'd left her. Relief washed over me. It was time to head back to Gary. I'd been in there for much longer than I anticipated.

As I walked outside, the sunlight pierced my eyes. I could hear nothing but the sounds of chirping birds. I knew it was safe to talk now that no one was around.

"Gary?" I called out.

I got no answer.

I walked toward the dumpster where Gary had been waiting. One of his shoes remained with a note attached.

FIRE AND PAIN,

19

WE MUST ENDURE TO GAIN.
YOUR PROBLEMS ARE DEEPER,
MR. TIME KEEPER.

___C___ Murphy's law was in full effect today, and I wasn't handling it very well.

In a fit of extreme anxiety, I unleashed the contents of my stomach all over the ground.

A lonely passerby took notice of my sudden sickness and was concerned.

"Are you feeling ill, sir? May I offer you something to drink?"

The man was probably in his late fifties, but living on the street had aged him much faster than normal. He had a dirty, grey beard that was nearly down to his waist. He presented a small tin canteen that appeared to have seen years of abuse.

I took a small swig. I nearly choked and spit out the liquid. The vagrant laughed briefly, then showed frustration over the lost contents.

"I'll have you know that this is the finest moonshine in all of D.C.! Try again with a little more dignity, and keep it down this time, or I'll regret ever stopping to help you."

This time I took a much smaller sip, and—true to his words—it tasted very fine, if such a word can be used to describe moonshine.

Feeling a little better, I thanked the man and bid him farewell.

"Be careful," the old man noted. "They say that killer is still on the loose! Rode off on horseback yesterday, and God only knows where he's hiding out."

I tipped my invisible hat to that and walked away.

Think, Jimmy. What is the next move here?

Shorting out the device without Gary would trap him in the past. I wasn't that desperate yet. After all, I was still alive, which meant that the future had not been altered *that* badly, if at all.

I re-examined the note to ensure I hadn't missed anything. Upon closer inspection, the parchment looked to be a piece of one of the posters for Our American Cousin. This means that whoever wrote this had recently been to the theater. I examined the ground around me for any sign of recent footprints. The area had been so heavily traveled the past few days that it was nearly impossible to distinguish old tracks from new ones.

That's when I noticed the blood. A few drops lingered two feet from where I found the note. I couldn't be sure whether or not the blood belonged to Gary. The drops continued, away from the scene.

___Z___ I walked the streets hoping to stumble upon some sort of clue as to Gary's whereabouts. The trail of blood continued into a dark alley. I was skeptical of it, but I figured if Gary was down there, I was his only hope.

My legs were shaky, and sweat began to rise from my skin. The alleyway seemed to grow colder as I followed the trail further and further. The sounds of the city became muffled, and buildings blocked the sunlight. My hackles rose as a wisp of air brushed the back of my neck. I turned around.

THUNK.

Six hours later

I awoke to pitch black and the smell of sour wine—again. I was sure I had been moved from where I was struck, but I had no idea where I was. I tried to stand up, but my limbs wouldn't move. I was bound to a chair.

Millions of thoughts ran through my mind, but Gary was at the forefront of them all. I had to find him, but first I had to find my way out of this situation. Quietly, I used my voice to determine the size of the room I was in.

"Hello?"

My prison couldn't have been too large, because my voice seemed to bounce back off of a wall immediately. Before I could say anything else, I heard a faint sound, like a small kitten trying to meow for the first time. Then, a faint cry for help. I froze.

"Gary?!"

I noticed the sound of footsteps outside the room, followed by the squeaking of door hinges. A dim light appeared just outside the door, but it was not quite bright enough to illuminate the face of the figure that held it.

A deep, scratchy, and familiar voice said, "Who is talking?"

The light brightened as I stared in the direction of the voice. Gary was lying in a puddle of blood with Grovtz hunched over him. A wave of anger surged through my pounding chest. My mind reeled. I began to think murderous thoughts toward Franklin Grovtz the Third.

I took in a deep breath, looked at Gary and (___C___) began laughing hysterically.

Grovtz did not appreciate my howling. His expression twisted into that of a boy trying his first piece of sour candy. He took a few steps forward and slapped my face with the back of his hand.

"Snap out of it, boy!" he said.

His sissy pimp-slap did nothing to calm my outrageous laughter. If anything, it made it worse.

Even in the dim light, I could see that Grovtz was beginning to turn a new shade of purple. He picked up a candlestick that was standing upright on a table about four feet away from me. Without giving me a chance to compose myself, he raised the candlestick and proceeded to worsen my already concussive state.

THUNK.

AS I SLID BACK into a state of consciousness, I rapidly noticed an excruciating amount of pressure in my skull.

This Grovtz character had apparently no knowledge of chronic traumatic encephalopathy. Of course, in this era, it had yet to be discovered, so he was probably innocent in this regard. However, common sense must allow most people to realize that clubbing another person on the shell that protects their brain cannot go without some sort of damage. Regardless, I was sure that Grovtz had an agenda of his own, and a part of that did not entail keeping me well preserved.

My awakening senses once again told me that I was in a dark room, likely the same one. But there was a different smell this time. The smell of burning flesh.

Not good.

I needed to formulate a game plan quickly. I tugged on the binds that locked my limbs into place, and—with actually no struggle at all—I was able to rip my arms free.

That was entirely too easy.

I freed one foot at a time, taking a mental note that this could be a trap. The string was no stronger than five-pound test fishing line that I would use to catch crappie on the lake when I was young.

I took a few steps forward and kicked a metallic object. I reached down through the darkness and grabbed it—the candlestick that had been acquainted with my skull.

I reached into my pocket and felt around for my lighter, which was surprisingly right where I had left it. Grovtz didn't even bother to check my pockets.

Amateur captor.

I felt around for my other belongings. Patting my chest, I realized he might not be the amateur I'd taken him for. GranGran was missing, *again!*

I lit the candle, opened the door to the room, and hurried toward the terrible smell coming from a few rooms down the hallway. There was a light emitting from under a door about twenty feet away.

A muffled voice yelled out in frustration, followed by a scream of agonizing pain. My hackles rose. A wooden chair lay on the ground across from me. I easily broke a leg off, careful to be as quiet as possible. I extinguished the candle flame between my fingers and crept toward the room, wielding the chair leg like a baseball bat.

I grabbed the door handle, took a deep breath, and swung it open.

___**Z**___ On the ground in front of my feet was a thick pool of dark red blood, lined with streaks of oil from a broken lamp next to it. A grotesque scene that lay ahead stood out as the definite source of the blood.

Like something out of a *Saw* movie, Gary was looming over what I assumed was the body of Grovtz. The corpse was so horribly disfigured that anyone could've mistaken it for a plate of barbecued pulled pork in the poor light of the room.

I looked up at Gary. He held an object, roughly the size of a baseball, in his right hand and was studying it. I figured it to be GranGran.

"Throw it here, Gary. I'll get us back," I said as normally as I could, my hands quivering.

He turned his head toward me and grinned widely. Laughing, he tossed it to me.

What landed in my hands was not GranGran. It was warm, wet, and tough like a piece of meat. I hardly needed to look to realize that this was the heart of Franklin Grovtz the Third.

Panic ensued, and I dropped the heart on the floor.

"*Gary!* What have you done? Do you know what you might have done to the future?"

Gary looked at me, his hair sopped with congealing blood. From the corner, he produced GranGran and shoved it in his coat pocket, all the while saying, "Fire and pain, we must endure to gain. Your problems are deeper, Mr. Time Keeper."

My heart sank, and my blood turned to ice. Gary reached into his pants pocket and pulled out a match.

I looked down at my feet, which were covered in blood and oil.

Gary struck the match once, twice. The sound was like a piece of paper slowly ripping.

I looked up at him. The world seemed to slow as a tear rolled down my cheek.

He dropped the match into the oil, and the flames spread quickly. Heat began biting at my legs. Taking one last look at me, he left the room and locked the door behind him.

Gary Barnige *betrayed* me.

___C___ *There's no way out,* I thought.

It was a nightmare come true.

Around the room, there were a few items that I could probably use to break open the door. But the spreading fire now consumed the only entry and exit to the room. I ran into the corner of the small room and crouched down to hug my knees. I figured this was the end. I had no method of escape. Any attempt at this stage would only be a faster means to an end.

A strange peace came over me. I knew that my death was inevitable, and so I accepted it. I thought about my life. Suddenly, my peace was replaced with regret.

What do I have to show for this miserable and lonely life that I have lived?

I closed my eyes and squeezed them tight. Smokey tears burned as they were purged from their ducts. I was suddenly aware that the room had now become silent.

Surprised, I opened my eyes.

My world stood still. Not even the flames had the power to move. As if I too was bound by the rules of this moment, I sat frozen and simply observed the stillness. The thought occurred to me that this might not last very long. I recalled how time stood still in the alley and remembered the fleeting nature of that moment.

Might I actually be able to escape?

I reached out and quickly moved my hand through the flames in front of me, testing the heat.

I felt nothing.

The fire danced strangely in the wake of my moving arm. But I was not burned. It hardly felt any different from the heat in the rest of the room. As an experiment, I held my hand in the flames, ready to pull it out at the slightest sign of burning. It was hot, but it did not burn my skin.

A voice from behind startled me. "The fire will not burn you right now, but it will if you don't come with me right this instant!"

The scare nearly knocked me onto the floor.

I spun around quickly.

Standing over me was a very pale, but beautiful woman in a strange suit. Something about her suit seemed not of this world. She held out her hand and gestured for me to take it.

Confusion froze me, and I could only stare and mutter fragments of words. She quickly realized I wasn't going to take her hand, so she grabbed me by the shirt and yanked me backward—through a wall. The world became brighter.

I was now seated on the floor of a room in which everything was unfamiliar. I felt the contents of my body begin to turn circles. I wretched, unleashing the contents of my stomach all over the white, polished floor.

Without warning, the woman who had saved me from the fire doubled over and vomited too. Then, she pulled two syringes from a pouch on her waist. She jammed one into her right leg and the other into my left thigh.

The vomiting ceased immediately, my innards stopped doing somersaults.

"What the heck was that about?" I asked, stunned.

"The syringe contained an antidote for T.A.P.E.."

"What is T.A.P.E.?"

"Time-Adjusting Persistent Emesis," she answered. "It happens when most organic life-forms move quickly through vast distances in time."

"Did we just time-travel?"

"Yes. I've been ordered to bring you in to speak to the Core. I know you don't know what that means right now, but I need you to trust me."

I looked around the room blankly, unable to reply.

"Look at me," the woman commanded. "You will have plenty of time to look around this place later, but right now we have lots to discuss. My identity is TEM-III/Zulu-Siiva Rommur. For brevity's sake, you can call me Siiva."

I blinked rapidly. "Sorry. This is all...weird. I...don't really know what to say, but...I'm Jimmy. Jimmy Truffle."

The woman called Siiva handed me a radiant orange pill and a glass of what appeared to be water.

"What is this?" I asked quizzically.

"It will help you to understand everything I am about to tell you. Do not take offense, but your mind is too feeble for such things. If allowed to process the information on your own, it would take too much precious time. Your people created this in your future to allow your kind to maximize its brainpower."

It felt as if something in my brain snapped loose. Like a cable under too much tension. "What do you mean 'my people'?" I questioned.

"Just take the medicine!" Siiva said impatiently.

She pushed the pill into my mouth and tilted the glass toward my face.

I swallowed and waited for some miraculous feeling to take me over.

After thirty seconds, I felt a sensation in my stomach, like bubbles popping. I stared blankly at the floor.

"Is that it? Did it work?"

I looked up at Siiva, who sat in a chair now, her arm raised as if checking a watch. Her eyes were fixed on a thin screen of numbers that were somehow emerging from her skin. Her mouth moved slightly as she concentrated. "Riiiiight about...now," she said matter-of-factly.

Immediately following her remark, it seized me. The air pressure seemed to increase drastically until I felt like the fist of God himself was constricting me.

Suddenly, I was hurled through space. The acceleration nearly caused me to black out—it must be what getting shot from a cannon feels like. The entire universe raced past me at incomprehensible speed...and then, more universes.

In those moments, I saw every passing of every event that has ever happened or ever will happen. I witnessed every version of reality and every possibility of events.

Past, present, and future folded into one another until nothing was left at all.

I halted suddenly, suspended in black, unable to perceive anything.

A thousand years seemed to pass as I floated undisturbed in the void. The only thing that I could sense was a whirring feeling inside my skull, as if my brain was spinning out of control.

After an indescribable amount of time, an aura emerged from the nothingness in front of me. It seemed gaseous, and liquid, and solid—yet somehow none of them at all.

I closed my eyes, and oddly enough, I could still see the being, as if my eyelids were made of glass.

More time passed, and then the aura began to pulse. Rapidly expanding and contracting, it seemed to be everywhere and nowhere in each instant. I was suddenly overwhelmed by massive waves of vibration that seemed to shake every atom in my body. There are no words that can describe the intensity or depth of the feeling.

The vibrations increased, growing ever more powerful, until I felt that I might violently explode.

Then, all was still once more.

4

JOPULOUS

___Z___ THE DARKNESS WAS calming; the emptiness, soothing. For once in my life, I had no worries. No thoughts crossed my mind, and no feelings possessed me.

As I floated in oblivion, I noticed particles beginning to form into a mass in front of me. Siiva appeared out of the mass and—without uttering a single syllable—asked me to follow her. I hadn't a clue or a care where we were going.

As we flew through the vacuum of space, I started to see small objects appear far below me. The speed of our travel blurred my vision so that I couldn't distinguish the objects from each other. From a distance, the objects appeared to be blobs of molten metal.

Slowly, I realized a city was materializing underneath me; massive buildings grew out of thin air, glowing as if they were stars.

Siiva spoke to me as we continued toward the city, but her mouth never moved. She was in my head, telling me the history of the realm: Jopulous, The City of a Thousand Planets.

I gazed at the metropolis in sheer amazement. Tall trees shielded the outskirts of the city from cosmic radiation from the three suns that loomed overhead. Waterfalls fell upward and trickled up the sides of large palaces that covered the streets with their vast shadows. This place was phenomenal. There was a likeness to human architecture and technology melded with other forms of design and creation that were unrecognizable to me. I would soon find out that the Vedren citizens lived in this paradise. It was incomparable to anywhere else in existence.

After a few minutes, I realized that Siiva's voice was still droning on in my head. I decided to pay attention in case I was missing anything important.

'You're probably wondering how a little settlement on the edge of the universe ended up becoming the beating heart of knowledge and tech, right? Well, Jimmy, Jopulous didn't just spring up overnight. It started small, just like everything does. But over the centuries, it became the central hub, all because of its alliances with a thousand different planets. Those allied planets are where Jopulous gets everything—the technologies, the wisdom, the innovation. They've been sharing their knowledge for millennia, and Jopulous became the vault where it all came together.'

"Wow!" I said aloud. I looked at everything below me and thought about all of the recent moments that had led up to this one.

Siiva's voice interrupted my thoughts, "We have arrived. Welcome to the Dome of the Ardent."

My feet touched down. A stretch of pearlescent road lay before us, leading to the massive dome. Beneath me, a glowing symbol pulsed with strange energy—a branch-like flame encircled by an ornate lace border. I couldn't help but feel drawn to it, captivated by its design. I felt an incredible warmth on my skin from the three suns overhead.

Siiva's smooth voice crept into my mind once again,

'Come with me, and don't say a word. The Vedren people aren't used to seeing your kind here.'

31

I swallowed a lump in my throat. We walked up the steps and stopped beneath two massive doors. The guardsmen of the Dome approached us and asked Siiva of our purpose. She reached into her waist belt and pulled out GranGran.

My mind raced.

How did she get that?

Using my newly acquired skill for telepathy, I asked,

'Siiva, what is going on? Are you going to explain anything to me?'

She ignored me, showing the time-altering device to the guards. They motioned us inside. In front of me were a thousand holographic planets, suspended in air, orbiting a small chair. Siiva and I slowly walked towards the chair and the holograms disappeared.

The guards glared at me suspiciously.

A titanic voice pierced the dome, "Liok Las Danibuh!"

Siiva looked at me informatively, "Kneel, Jimmy. He is here."

Confused, I asked, "Who?"

Siiva pulled me to my knees and whispered, "The Ardent of Jopulous, Serda Holiq."

The dome grew quiet as Holiq made his way to his chair. The wooden chair seemed too simple for the Ardent, but I decided it was not my place to judge. He sat down and cleared his throat.

"Jimmy Truffle, (___C___) I am Serda Holiq, the Ardent of Jopulous and Protector of this observable universe. You are very far from home. It seems that you have unknowingly flown too close to the sun, as your kind might say. You are familiar with your species' story of Icarus, are you not?"

The Ardent stared down from his chair in silence, awaiting my response.

The entire situation was bewildering to me, but somehow, in this moment, everything seemed to be strangely normal. I supposed that I must have undergone some bizarre change when I was in the presence of the aura. I had yet to look at myself since the "change" occurred to see if my physical appearance had been altered.

I met the Ardent's gaze with a calm demeanor, "I have heard of the story you speak of."

A brutish figure to the Ardent's left barked, "You will address the Ardent as 'Your Sovereignty!'"

Before I could correct myself, Ardent Holiq intervened. "You need not use such formalities, Time Keeper."

I searched through the vast amount of information that I had recently absorbed to find an explanation for this 'Time Keeper' phrase that I kept hearing. There were still many things that did not make sense to me.

The Ardent spoke back up. "I can see that you have a lot of questions, and they shall be answered soon enough, but there are some things that I must tell you first."

The aged being appeared small and frail, but in his stormy eyes could be seen the power and vitality of a whole city of men. His voice was soft but aggressive. He spoke every word matter-of-factly. His face bore no expression. He held a staff in his hand that appeared to be made of a polished wood, only there was a glowing orb at the crown that shone with a pale, blue light.

"You have opened a gateway into time. Such a thing has never been accomplished by a Type-One civilization. Word of this has reached the dark beings of our Universe. They are calling you 'Time Keeper', and it seems to me that you might be such."

I looked to Siiva, kneeling on my left, for clarification. She only nodded her head toward the Ardent, who then continued, "However impressive your invention and ability, you were very naïve before Siiva sent you to meet the Core, and the ripples of your actions have stirred up a big mess. The planet that you have come from—known to us as W-729—has experienced some terrible effects from your disturbance of its past. As the Protector of the Observable Universe, it is my duty to aid your planet and bring balance back to your civilization. This is no easy task, but I have a plan that will undoubtedly work, as long as I have your full cooperation."

The Ardent then turned his head to the giant seated to his right, "General, please explain."

The large figure stood up slowly and addressed me with a booming voice, "Time Keeper, I am General Krael, the Commander of the Armies of Jopulous. Ardent Holiq has assigned me to guide you on your quest to undo your mistakes. There are dark and terrible things in the Unobservable Universe that prey on inexperienced time-travelers like yourself. Mortal beings do not possess the ability to speak their real names, but the Vedren people call them Leeches. When you repeatedly opened rifts to the past in your dimension, you got the attention of the Leeches. One of them, known to us as Boral, took on the appearance of your friend Gary. When he stole the device you call 'GranGran', I sent Siiva to take it back from him.

"Boral has returned to his realm for now, but he will be back. When he returns, we need to be ready for a fight. A massive army of Leeches will likely accompany him. They have a special interest in your GranGran device. We need your help to find out why. As its creator, you know more about it than anyone else. In return for your help, the Ardent wishes to offer you a life eternal in Jopulous."

I gulped at that last mind-bending sentiment.

The General continued. "Tonight, we will provide you with accommodations and allow you to consider our proposal. Siiva will show you to your room and answer all of your questions. We will convene again this time tomorrow to hear your response."

With that, we stood at once and departed.

Siiva walked briskly past me.

"Follow me."

___Z___ As we walked down a long corridor toward the Dome's guest rooms, Siiva turned to me with a grin. "Do you have any questions?"

"Actually, yes. Where are the beds?" I asked, feeling utterly exhausted from recent events.

She snickered. "You are in for a rude awakening, Mr. Truffle. Let's go. We are almost to your room."

After a few more minutes of walking, we stopped at an old wooden door that looked different from all the other doors in the hall. The door seemed to awaken dormant memories.

"Look familiar?" Siiva asked. "This is the door of the house you grew up in. The Vedren people hold the past in the highest regard—and your planet, too. That's why they're so determined to protect it. They believe doors are physical symbols of life's most important truths. Doors open our minds to new experiences. They are gateways to change and new beginnings. You're ready for a new life, Jimmy. Go ahead. Open the door."

I turned the cold glass knob, pushed the door open, and stared at my new living quarters; a vacant room, no bigger than a large walk-in closet.

"Don't worry," Siiva said. "This room can be as big and as full of life as you desire. You just have to learn how to use your powers."

Frustrated, I asked, "What powers? Can you please explain all of this to me?"

She sat silently.

I thought to myself that Siiva must have been trying to get me riled up, but after a few moments, she began explaining the current circumstances to me. The eleven-minute conversation left me with two concrete answers.

The first is that I had become a Hudren. This half-Vedren, half-human subspecies was initially created to spy on Earth. They appear, act, and sound completely human, but have all the abilities of a Vedren. There are only a few of us.

The second thing that I learned is that the Vedren powers I have gained are slightly limited in comparison to those of a true Vedren, but are impressive nonetheless. Upon meeting the Core, I was given a portion of three Vedren powers: telepathy, the ability to travel inter-dimensionally without cellular collapse, and cerebral solid creation (CSC). All are pretty self-explanatory, except for the latter. CNC is basically just the power to create any solid object out of thin air by simply saying the object's name out loud.

"Strawberry." I took a bite.

Pretty much at this point, I realized that I am kind of a big deal!

After finally putting an end to my gargantuan state of confusion and injecting me with a confidence I never knew existed, Siiva turned to walk out of the room.

"Wait up!" I yelled.

"What is it, Jimmy?"

I looked around my room, "Ummmm, where is my bed again?"

Siiva laughed, "I forgot to mention that Hudren are unable to sleep due to the cross-DNA influx pulses we get now and then."

I was scared to ask, but I did it anyway. "What are those?"

"They're pretty much just massive seizure that we will have at least twice a day. No worries though, it only *feels* like you're dying; you won't *actually* die," she explained playfully.

Now fearing for my life, I asked her what I was supposed to do instead of sleeping.

"I usually stare at the wall or use CSC to create new species of life and then send them to a new planet. It's a pretty fun pastime. I'll bring the dinosaurs back one day; mark my words!" she laughed. "Anyway, see you tomorrow, Jim. We have a lot of planning to do."

As she exited the room, I thought about how much I liked the Hudren who had kidnapped me and brought me to this strange place. I thought about how strikingly gorgeous she was. I remembered my newly acquired powers, and I smirked as I thought about what sort of things I could create tonight.

I imagined making a copy of Siiva. I nearly tried, but then I realized it would be hard to hide it from the real Siiva.

5

Fire and Pain

___C___ I WAITED FOR the inevitable seizures, spending the next several hours listening to my heart beating rhythmically inside my chest.

Thump thump...Thump thump...Thump thump.

The sound stole me away into a trance-like state. For some time, I relaxed on the bed that I had created with my new powers. I still needed a lot of practice with my CSC precision. The bed felt slightly lumpy, like clumps of flour in a batter that did not get mixed well enough. Nevertheless, it would do.

My brain felt exhausted from the past few days. There was just too much new information to process. This act of lying in silence, meditating upon each beat of my heart, was the only thing that I wanted to do until Siiva returned.

A moment later, as if the thought alone summoned her, she walked into the room.

I sprang quickly to my feet. "Haven't you heard of knocking?!" I asked, surprised.

A puzzled look came over her face. "What?"

I realized then that she actually might not know. "Usually, where I come from, people knock on the door to alert the person inside that they are coming in."

This didn't seem to change the puzzled expression on her face.

"Why would you need to know when I am coming in? Am I not welcome inside?"

I exhaled deeply and rubbed the bridge of my nose.

"No. I mean, yes, you are welcome, it's just...this is my private sanctuary, and I need my privacy."

Siiva seemed appeased with this explanation.

"As you wish. In the future, I shall knock. Did you sleep much?"

I stared at her blankly. "Uuuum, no! You said that we *couldn't* sleep."

She burst into laughter. "It was a *joke!* Do you not have humor in your culture?"

"What? Yes!" I answered, a little perplexed.

"Okay," she said. "Now, please sit in this **chair** and let's try to come up with a plan."

When she uttered the word chair, a black stool appeared underneath her hands, which were held facedown in front of her stomach. She slid in front of me.

Another stool appeared perpendicular to mine. Siiva sat down in this one. Following her lead, I took my seat. A table formed in front of us, and she leaned over it.

"Wait, how did you make your chair and the table appear without speaking the words?" I asked.

She turned her gaze toward me and smiled. "It will take time, but you will eventually master your new abilities. For now, you need to speak the words aloud to tune yourself to the vibratory patterns of the creative ether. Soon you will be able to translate your thoughts into instructions for the invisible forces that you command."

Boy, I have a lot to learn! I thought.

Siiva pulled a small black box from a pocket on her suit. She opened the box and removed what appeared to be a giant ballpoint pen. She held it to my arm, as if to write something. Suddenly, I felt a sting under my skin.

"What was that?" I exclaimed, pulling my arm quickly away and staring at a small pinhole, where a tiny droplet of blood was taking shape.

"That's your personal monitor." Siiva explained. "It will display the current time in whatever location you are in, assuming a time zone exists in that place. It can help you navigate to any destination in the multiverse. It will monitor your health, and it can also assist with the execution of certain tasks."

I touched the spot on my arm, which now looked like a large freckle. A small hologram emerged with a multitude of symbols that I did not understand.

As I stared in awe, Siiva added, "You can also use it to Google things."

I stared at her, trying to figure out if she was joking. "Are you serious? You people have the godly ability to talk inside each other's heads; to move and create things with your mind, and yet, you are using human technology!?"

My words came out louder than I expected, but Siiva did not seem bothered.

"Not originally human technology, if you must know," Siiva remarked bluntly. "It is *Gliggorian* technology. The Gliggorians willingly gave it to your NASA when they simultaneously visited your moon."

I closed my eyes and massaged my temples. If my brain hadn't been recently "upgraded", I might have a splitter headache right now.

"Okay, whatever. But did you have to inject it into my arm? It feels weird. Couldn't you just install it into a bracelet or ring or something?"

"There is a reason for everything, Jimmy. Your chip will help us to identify you if you are slaughtered in the coming battle. If it were in a piece of jewelry and that were lost, how would we tell you apart from any other person from your world?"

I slapped my knees in surprise. "Are you trying to say that everybody from Earth looks the same?"

Siiva seemed to be getting frustrated. "We are getting off-topic. Please focus for a moment. Boral has returned to his dimension, and he will be amassing an army to return for the GranGran device. We don't have time to figure out why they want this device so badly. We need to formulate a plan of attack. A Leech cannot enter Jopulous unless they are escorted by one of the Vedren people. So, we are safe in here, but they will still come, and they will wait outside for as long as they must."

I thought to myself briefly, and then said, "Why must we attack if we are safe in here? Why don't we just stay here until they go away?"

"Jimmy, they know that they cannot enter Jopulous, but they will wait for us to travel beyond our safety net, and they will pick us off one by one. Leeches are timeless creatures. They will wait for all eternity for us to leave our boundaries. We cannot all remain inside forever. Many Vedren have entire galaxies that they are cultivating outside our own, and they must tend to them, or they will fail. You, yourself, have a friend who needs your help. You must go to him soon. He may prove himself to be of great value in your journey."

I gasped loudly.

I forgot all about Gary! He must be frantic! Lost in the past. Searching helplessly for me. Unable to return to the present. Wait...am I still in the past? I thought.

As if I were speaking aloud, Siiva interjected, "You are in a place where time moves so slowly that it hardly exists. Hardly a moment has passed in Earth time. The room I pulled you out of has not burned any more than it had before you left it. If a hair had fallen from your head when I jerked you, it would have hardly fallen its length toward the floor by now. But technically, we're in the future—at least from the perspective of the time you just came from—so time doesn't really matter. You can always go back to where you left off later if you want."

This seemed to calm my fears for the moment. I adjusted myself to feel more comfortable in my seat and refocused my thoughts on the task at hand.

"So, if we must attack the Leeches, how can they be defeated?" I asked.

"We are still trying to figure that out. We now know only that the Leeches are weak when they are alone. They are small creatures and not particularly powerful, but they have strength in numbers. Like a colony of Earth ants."

"So, we just need some bug spray!" I joked.

Siiva smiled at this. "If only it were that simple!"

I tapped the magic freckle on my arm that controlled my monitor. I stared at the symbols, trying to decipher them. In the corner of the display, I noticed something interesting.

"What is this?" I asked, pointing at the letters and numbers.

"That is your identity: TEM-I/Alpha-Jimmy Truffle. 'TEM' means that you have control over time in some way. The 'I' denotes the status of the civilization that you hail from. Earth is a Type One civilization, meaning that it has not yet fully utilized the energy provided by its central star. 'Alpha' shows your level of ability to perform your skills. The scale uses your phonetic alphabet, which also has its uses in our language. Essentially, you are a level-one player in this game, and you have a lot to learn. Your monitor tracks your skills, and your level of ability will be automatically updated. Of course, you should already know the remainder of your identity."

I stared at my identity. My name. I thought about Siiva's identity: TEM-III/Zulu-Siiva Rommur. I noticed that our beginning titles were the same. The next part had me baffled.

"Siiva, you are a *Zulu!* Does that mean you are the highest level?"

"Not quite," she replied. "There are a few levels after Zulu that can only be gifted to you by an Ardent or the Core itself—the master encoder of the Multiverse—which you have met."

At that moment, a sharp pain shot up my leg. I reached down instinctively to feel the limb. It was oddly swollen. I lifted the leg of my suit, which had been gifted to me by the Vedren. There was a giant bubble moving under my skin.

Siiva gasped. "We have to leave. *Now!*"

___**Z**___ FOR A WHILE, I drifted in and out of consciousness.

I finally returned to myself under the bright lights of a hospital room. Siiva walked in, as if my waking cued her entry.

"How are you feeling, Jimmy?"

"I feel fine. What happened to me?" I asked.

She sat down on the foot of my bed.

"You had a Leech inside your leg, Jim. It found its way into your bloodstream during your last time-travel. This is a very rare occurrence, and it is also very dangerous. You are lucky you only lost one leg."

I smiled at her and let out a sigh of relief...then it hit me.

I panicked and screamed in disbelief, *"Lost one leg!?"*

My arms set a new speed record as I ripped the sheets off my lower body. I counted multiple times, just to be sure. Both legs seemed to be intact.

"Siiva, never, ever scare me like that again!"

She laughed hysterically.

I beamed at her with a disgusted expression.

"Are you gonna keep pestering me, or will you tell me what happened to the Leech?"

Squeezing out her last few chuckles, Siiva explained that the Leech died while the surgeons were extracting it from my leg. That was unfortunate because the Vedren scientists wanted to study the Leech as it developed into an adult. But such is life.

"Well, what is the plan now?" I asked Siiva.

"You need to go find your friend, Gary. I will be here studying the dead Leech. I think I might be able to create a replica with a few special mutations using CNC. If I can do this, Jimmy, we might have the ultimate weapon against the Leech army. One of their own." Siiva stood up and headed toward the door. "Don't put any pressure on that leg until it heals. Shouldn't be more than a few hours, okay? Go and find Gary as soon as you can. We will need everyone we can muster to defeat the Leeches. I may or may not be back before you have the chance to leave."

She walked out and closed the door behind her.

My mind raced as I lay back onto my pillow. Things were becoming pretty overwhelming.

Keep it together, Jimmy. Gary needs you, I thought.

Three hours later

I was about halfway through a good holographic book called *Even Shadows Have Shadows* when I felt my leg twitch. I looked down at it. The gnarly rip in my flesh had closed in mere hours.

These powers are nothing to shake a stick at, I thought.

I gazed around the room. My outfit was draped over a floral chair in the corner.

Before I could stand to retrieve it, the floor began to shake and a rumbling noise echoed in the near distance.

CRASH BANG BLAM BOOM!

The door to my room flew from its hinges and careened toward my head. I ducked, avoiding decapitation by mere inches.

After the dust cleared, I looked up to see Siiva standing over me.

"What in San Paolo was *that!?*" I yelled in total shock.

She looked at me, confused. "I was just *knocking*, Jimmy. Isn't that what you asked me to do?"

Face, meet Palm.

I couldn't even be mad at her. Though I wouldn't say it aloud, I did find it a bit humorous, only given that I wasn't dead. The door had occupied a hole in the hospital wall that now gave way to a gorgeous view of the distant Jopulous Gardens.

I stood up and asked Siiva why she came back.

"I just wanted to let you know, " she started, "that the Galactic War Organization has recruited me to partake in a series of meetings to discuss the upcoming fight with the Leech Army. I will be there for a week, and then I will return to Jopulous to hopefully create our new Leech friend from the specimen in your leg. I think that could help us win this war. You won't have me holding your hand when you return to find Gary, so be careful. See you soon, Jimmy."

Siiva walked out, and I put on my suit.

I'm coming for you, Gary!

___C___ I REALIZED QUICKLY that I hadn't the slightest clue how to get back to 1865 on Earth. Siiva hadn't exactly given me a walkthrough on using my newly acquired powers. I exited my quarters and walked around looking for someone to ask for directions.

After some wandering, I found my way into a garden of strange but incredible flowers. I stopped for a second to gaze at a large orange plant. It looked similar to a giant sunflower; only the colors were different, and the head of the plant was floating above its stem. It hung suspended in thin air above the bulbous leaves below.

"Hruuvol, or 'hover weed' in your lan-ua-e," a voice said.

I turned to get a glimpse of the owner of the voice, who was standing about twenty feet away. The thing had enormous eyes, resembling a fly's. He had one leg and three arms on each side of his body. He was dressed differently from many of the other Vedren. I turned my attention back to the plant and swished my hand back and forth under the hovering flower.

"How does it do that?" I asked.

The man-fly-thing laughed, "You understand ma-netism, do you not?"

I shook my head. "Do you mean, magnetism?"

It nodded. "I apolo-ize, but I am physically incapable of pronouncin- the sound of that letter. By the way, my name is Nurii-nar. I am the caretaker of the sacred Jopulous -ardens. Almost all of the plants in the observable universe are present here. The -ardens take up three theks, or over five thousand square miles on your planet."

I looked around, puzzled. The gardens looked to be only an acre or two.

"How is that possible?" I asked. "It looks no bigger than a football field."

Nuriignar scratched his head, "I'm not sure what a football is, but there is much more to the –ardens than meets the eye."

He raised what I assumed to be his eyebrows and used all of his arms to point down.

"Underground?" I asked.

He nodded.

"Cool. Well, can you tell me how to find General Krael, or the Ardent?" I asked politely.

Nuriignar motioned for me to approach.

When I had made it within an arm's length, he grabbed me by the sleeves with four arms and pulled me close to him.

Is this fly-man-thing trying to hug me right now? I thought.

He pulled my forehead into his chest. Having nothing covering the upper half of his chest, my head could feel the interesting texture of his skin. It was a bit cold and much too slimy for my comfort.

I pulled away as delicately as I could, trying not to offend him. Then, I realized his intention.

He had somehow uploaded the information to me.

Minutes ago, I had been lost, but now I could intuitively see the path to every building, as if I had walked the roads of Jopulous all my life.

I looked up at Nuriignar's bug-like face and smiled.

"You are welcome, Time Keeper," he said, even though I had not verbally thanked him yet.

I turned toward the Dome of the Ardent, where I would have to go to meet the General again.

"Thanks!" I said, belatedly, "but, I'm still not sure why everyone keeps calling me 'Time Keeper?'"

I turned back toward Nuriignar, hoping for an answer, but he was no longer there.

"Probably tending to the under-round plants," I said to myself, chuckling.

The Dome of the Ardent was a massive structure. Hundreds of feet tall, it was grey and it seemed from a distance to be constructed of concrete, but—upon closer inspection—the material that made up the Dome was some type of semi-solid substance. The surface was smooth and maintained its shape, but it was constantly moving, swirling around, like the blobs inside a lava lamp. I brushed my hand across the surface of the wall. The material repelled my hand. It felt to me like another hand had reached through the wall and pushed my hand away.

Strange, but cool!

I entered the Dome through the large doors in front, which were opened by the guards, who clearly recognized me this time. General Krael was seated next to the Ardent, where we last spoke. I approached the leaders of this bizarre world. The General and the Ardent sat up taller in their chairs as I arrived in front of them. I knelt to show my respect.

"Time Keeper, are you well today?" asked the Ardent.

"I am well," I responded, "but can someone please explain why everyone keeps calling me that?"

The Ardent stared out toward the horizon for a few brief moments before replying.

"Jimmy Truffle, I am glad to hear that you are well. Have you had time to consider my proposal?"

I took a moment to recall the previous day's conversation.

The proposal? Of course! I was supposed to deliver my answer today.

"It's a lot to think about," I started, "but I don't suppose I have any other choice. Now, about my question..."

I darted my eyes back and forth between the two leaders.

General Krael spoke up next, "Explaining who you are is not our job. Boral refers to you as such, and Boral is observant and intelligent beyond imagination. If you do not already know, you will have to ask him; although, I don't expect you will have the opportunity. Please note that, for reasons unknown to you at this time, we believe this title suits you well. Now, you must give us your answer to the proposal."

I sighed in frustration and ran my fingers through my hair.

"I've been through a lot in the past few days, and my memory is so clouded with thoughts that I cannot understand exactly what my role is in this predicament."

The Ardent sat forward in his chair and spoke. "You created this device that you call GranGran. Boral is adamant about getting his hands on it. We cannot fathom how he will use it, but we know his every intent is malicious from our perspective. You must learn more about the Leeches and help us figure out what they could possibly use it for."

Sounds easy enough.

"I will help you," I said, "but I have a few questions and conditions."

The General's eyebrows raised.

"Go on," he muttered impatiently.

I cleared my throat. "Well, first of all, I need to know if I'm in any danger."

"You are in no danger from the Leeches so long as you remain in Jopulous, Jimmy Truffle," Krael assured me.

I stood up, suddenly aware that I was still kneeling.

"Well, you said that already, but I've just come from your hospital, where a Leech was removed from my leg!"

General Krael raised his voice. "*You* brought that vermin here!"

"*Silence!*" the Ardent shouted. His voice resonated throughout the dome. "I believe you are innocent of transporting the Leech through our barriers, as it was unknown to you. We have scanned your body, and the danger has been eliminated. We have implanted a small device in you that will prevent Leeches from entering your body in the future. Anytime that you are outside of our barriers, you will be under the protection of Aair, Siiva's brother. He will escort you everywhere and ensure that your life is not in danger."

Relieved at this comment, I continued, "Okay. Well, what are the time constraints for this mission?"

The Ardent turned his gaze to the General, who replied, "We believe that the Leeches are amassing an army as we speak, and our sources gather that an attack is imminent before the rising of our moon."

I blinked rapidly, insinuating the need for elaboration.

A voice spoke up from behind me, startling me. "Sixty-seven weeks, in Earth-terms, sir."

I turned around to see a pale, white figure. He looked eerily similar to Siiva. "Forgive me for startling you, Time Keeper," the man said. "You may call me Aair. It is my job to oversee the safeguarding of W-729. I have recently been appointed to your protection, as well. We have much work to do, sir."

The General spoke once more, "Time is of the essence, Jimmy Truffle. What are your aforementioned conditions?"

I turned back around to face the prominent figure. "I know that time is short, but I have lost contact with my very dear friend, Gary. I must return to Earth and find him. I wish to have his help through this endeavor, and—assuming we succeed in defeating the Leeches—I would only like to stay in Jopulous if Gary is also permitted to stay. You would love him. He bakes incredible tea biscui..."

The General waved his hand, gesturing for me to stop talking. He and the Ardent then exchanged muffled words in a language that was foreign to me.

I turned to Aair for translation. He shrugged.

The language must have been a secret, because no one else in the room seemed to understand. The conversation dragged on for a tiny eternity.

When it finally stopped, there was a long pause as the two men pondered whatever they had spoken about.

My attention drifted to the sounds outside the Dome. There was a peaceful sound of water flowing full of life in the distance. There were also many sounds of strange machinery. The sounds of the city were unlike those of Earth, yet they filled me with an intriguing sense of belonging.

The conversation resumed between the General and the Ardent. The Ardent uttered something that I could not quite make out, but his words seemed to infuriate the General. Krael's voice rose to a shout, and he seemed to tremble as he spoke.

The Ardent shifted his eyes to meet mine.

The General continued to shout.

Suddenly, the Ardent raised his staff and slammed it into the ground. Every atom in the building shook, and a powerful blast of blue light pierced the Dome, temporarily blinding everyone present.

"General Krael, you have served me well for millennia. I do not devalue your opinion, but if you *ever* raise your voice in my direction again, I will banish you to the Void for the next millennium."

Powerful intention charged Ardent Holiq's words, and everyone in the room could feel it tangibly in the air.

The General dropped to his knees before the Ardent.

"Forgive me, Your Sovereignty."

The Ardent looked down on Krael with pity, and then gazed once more at me.

"I will allow you one month to find your friend, but no longer. Do not forget, time will pass quickly while you are there. You may be away for only a short time, but when you return, you may be surprised at how much time has passed. Use every moment wisely. My council will assess this man, Gary. If they deem him fit to help us, he will be allowed to do so. Upon successful completion of your mission, I will permit you both to reside among us."

I smiled and opened my mouth to speak, but was interrupted by the Ardent.

"*However*, if Gary, or you, for that matter, ever bring harm to my people or our way of life, I will ensure an *unimaginable* punishment comes to you. Is that understood?"

I swallowed a lump in my throat. "Crystal clear, Your Sovereignty."

"Good," he said. "Now, go find your friend."

Upon ending his sentence, the Ardent stood and pointed the ball of his staff in my direction. With a sharp jab to my chest, he propelled me through time and space.

MOMENTS LATER, I WAS lying with my back on a dusty floor. Familiar sounds and smells enlivened my sensory receptors.

I was back on Earth.

___Z___ I had been transported to what appeared to be a storage room. Huge wooden crates labeled *Eileen's Peanuts* hugged the mold-stained walls.

A soft voice behind me interrupted the silence. "Assessing time, date, and location: 0936, April 17th, 1865. Madame Tusan's Diner, Washington D.C.."

Startled, I turned around to identify the source of the voice. It was Aair, my newly assigned companion, whom I had already forgotten about.

"Thanks for that, Aair."

"No problem, sir," he said with a childish smirk.

I shook my head. "Please, call me Jimmy."

Aair stared at me as if he had never been given such first-name privileges.

"Yes, sir, Jimmy," he replied.

Siiva is definitely the more intimidating of the two, I thought to myself.

"We have to change clothes. Aair, you have CSC, correct?"

"Oh, do I?" he shouted.

A fluorescent green suit instantly appeared over his Vedren cloak.

"Are you sure you want to wear that? Doesn't it stand out too much?" I asked.

Aair spun around like a wannabe Michael Jackson.

"One thing I've learned in my five hundred and thirty-seven years, sir, is to always hide in plain sight."

"Whatever floats your boat," I replied. I used my creative powers to conceal my alien attire with a more time-period-appropriate suit.

I motioned Aair to the back exit.

"Let's go find Gary."

I never realized how filthy the air on Earth could be until that moment I stepped outside. Maybe it was my heightened senses or just trash-day eve, but—*holy Leech*—it reeked!

The streets were bustling with activity more than they were during my previous visit. The haze of the assassination seemed to have lifted. Children ran through the streets, and horses nearly trampled them. Strangely, no one looked overly concerned for the children's safety.

Aair and I walked through crowds of people and busy markets, looking for any sign of Gary.

Several passersby shot awkward glances at Aair's vibrant attire.

"Aair. You're drawing *way* too much attention to us with that outfit," I whispered.

Aair looked a bit sad, but he nodded in agreement. He found a sheltered spot between two buildings and quickly changed into clothes that wouldn't stand out.

"Happy now?" he asked, seeming a little perturbed.

I laughed, and we carried on.

The wind hurled a young voice our way. "Extra! Extra! Read all about it!"

A newspaper stand. Perfect.

As we walked towards the booth, a red-haired boy ran up to us. "Could I interest you in the daily paper, sirs?"

I smiled and replied, "Well, of course, young lad." I dug in my right pocket. "I know I had **ten dollars** in here earlier." Ten dollars appeared in my right hand.

I thought, *My, how CSC comes in handy.*

"Here you go, son, and keep the change."

The boy's eyes widened as he handed over the newspaper. I grabbed it, and not a second later, he sprinted around the corner shouting, "I'm rich! I'll never work again!"

"Won't be rich for long if you keep yelling that, boy," Aair mumbled.

I snickered and began scanning the paper for any evidence on Gary's whereabouts.

--Oldest Man Dies at Seventy-Eight!,
page 2

--Bad Cheese? Whole City Becomes
Sick, page 5

Spotting a promising headline, I flipped through the paper until I landed on it.

Fire at Aberdean Warehouse. Famed theater manager, Franklin Grovtz, was lost in the flames.

"Look, Aair, this article is about what Gary did when that Leech possessed him," I pointed out.

He peered over my shoulder and squinted to read. "This was written by a guy named Reginald Hanson, sir. Maybe if we find him, he can tell us where Gary is."

I nudged Aair on the shoulder. "That's a great start! Now, we just need the address."

I looked through the paper and stumbled upon Hanson News Emporium. I poked my arm's digital freckle and asked it to steer me toward the news station. It was a few miles away.

"C'mon, Aair. We aren't too far from it."

"Are we *walking* there?"

I was a little surprised. "Yes...it's not *that* far."

"But, we could just use a portal and be there in seconds," he said unenthusiastically.

I chuckled. "Don't you guys exercise on your planet?"

"I suppose so, sir. We usually get our exercise in the form of sword-fighting, grappling, and other combat-related activities. We tend to travel more efficiently when the activity is mundane and time is of the essence," Aair replied nonchalantly.

I raised my eyebrows, thinking about myself participating in physical combat. It seemed antithetical to my passive nature.

"Well, I like walking. It helps me clear my head," I remarked.

"Fair enough, sir," Aair conceded.

As we walked, I noticed a large owl that seemed to be following us. It's eyes tracked our every move.

I tried not to think about it too hard. I looked at Aair. My companion seemed all too quiet.

"Is everything alright, Aair?" I asked.

He took a deep breath. "I keep thinking about your friend Gary, sir—wondering if he'll be accepted."

I was confused. "What do you mean by that?"

He shook his head. "Sir, Gary was possessed by a Leech, correct?"

I nodded.

"Well, any form of life that gets possessed by a Leech becomes half-Leech. Some cases are good, while others are terrible. Let's hope your friend got lucky."

The remainder of the trip was spent in silence as I thought the worst for Gary.

"HERE WE ARE, SIR," Aair said as he knelt to give his legs a rest.

I looked up at the building. It was newly painted, a soothing shade of red that seemed welcoming. We walked inside. The smell of fresh ink filled the air. At a desk sat an elderly receptionist.

"Hello ma'am," I began respectfully, "is there any way we can speak to Mr. Hanson?"

"Oh yes, dear. He's in his office now. Just knock before you enter," the old woman replied.

I smiled and thanked the woman. I knocked loudly on the door, reminding me of Siiva's knock that nearly took my head off. I chuckled. I noticed a shadow moving underneath the door. It opened, revealing a much younger face than I anticipated. This man couldn't have been a day over twenty-two.

"May I help you, gentlemen?" he inquired.

"Yessir, my name is Jimmy Truffle, and this here is my good friend, Aair. We would like to know the current whereabouts of our friend, who was just recently involved in one of your stories."

Mr. Hanson opened the door wider and welcomed us inside, paying special attention to Aair's strange appearance.

This man could talk the face off of Mount Rushmore, so I'll spare you the dialogue, assuming that no one cares to spend three hours reading about how Roswell ink sits better on paper than Judfor ink. The pertinent information was as follows:

Gary was at Finley Hospital on North Grandview Avenue, recovering from severe dehydration and carbon monoxide poisoning. And...that's it. Everything else we learned was about stupid quill-pen ink.

Aair and I caught a horse and buggy to make the trip. The ride was bumpy and the driver was quite rude, but we arrived after no time at all. I was anxious to see Gary.

When we arrived at our destination, we hopped off the buggy and approached the hospital. It was old and rundown.

We walked inside and up to the visitors' desk. A young lady asked for our information and sent us up to Gary's room.

Before knocking, I stood outside the door, thinking the worst had happened to my dear friend.

I thought it best to caution Aair, "Stay outside for now, Aair. I don't know how Gary will react to seeing either of us."

Aair nodded and sat down on a nearby bench.

I faced the door and prepared for the worst.

Knock, knock.

A surprisingly gleeful voice sprang from inside, "Come in!"

I opened the door and—my golly—there he was: Gary Barnige, in the flesh, looking as healthy as ever.

"Master Truffle!" Gary yelled with excitement.

I ran over to his bedside. He beamed with joy.

"How are you doing, Gary?" I asked.

"I'm great, sir! I healed up real quick after the fire, and I've just spent the last day resting and gathering up my strength."

"Do you feel any...different?" I asked in a careful, inquisitive tone.

"Well, I wanted to wait and tell you, sir, but I'm half-Leech. I know everything about the Leech army, everything about your new powers, and I have some Leech powers in me now, sir."

Aair walked into the room and noted, "He got lucky, sir."

Gary leapt from his bed, startled by the sight of my companion. His arms transformed into long, green tentacles.

I ran towards him. "Whoa, whoa, *whoa!* Gary! Calm down. That's Aair. He's here to help us."

Gary looked at me. His eyes were filled with black smoke, and veins protruded from his neck.

A few moments of silence passed before Gary quickly dropped to a knee and returned to his human appearance. I grabbed his arm to help him onto his feet.

"I'm assuming that is one of your Leech abilities, Gary?"

"Yes, sir! Cool, right?" he remarked with pride.

He walked over to Aair and apologized.

Aair laughed off the scare and told Gary to save that wrath for Boral.

I interrupted the laughter. "Now that we have everyone accounted for, shall we be off to Jopulous?"

Aair smiled and nodded. Gary grabbed his belongings. Aair then pulled out his travel beacon and set it on the floor in front of us.

I eyed his new device and ventured to ask, "What is that, Aair?"

He rubbed his palms together. "It's my travel beacon!"

"Can't you just whip us up a portal without using a device?" I asked, laughing.

He looked sheepishly at me, but then replied, "I just like changing it up every now and then, sir. This one requires cool words, which I always like saying, but aren't very necessary anymore. Old Myst language!"

"Okay, no worries. I was just wondering," I consoled.

Looking at Gary, Aair telepathically gave him the words to allow for group travel.

Gary looked like he had stage-fright all of the sudden.

"Go ahead. After all you've been through, you deserve to say them." Aair commented.

Gary cleared his throat. "Serifus, aduti, jiklen!"

6

THE COUNCIL OF THE VALKYRIE

___C___ I WATCHED AS Gary spoke the words that would allow him to join us in our fast travel back to Jopulous.

The air became still.

For a moment, Gary was frozen in his animation. Human atoms take slightly longer to transition through dimensions than those of a Vedren or Hudren.

I studied his face. His expression reminded me of an old portrait that I had seen hanging on the wall in my mother's house. The old painting was of a Roman General. A great battle was about to begin, and the General was speaking to inspire courage in his men on the battlefield. Gary's face bore that same expression of confidence; however, he let slip a slight hint of emotion that the General must have shared during his moment in history.

Fear.

Gary had seen the enemy for what it truly was. His body shook with reanimation as his atoms finally adjusted to the fast-travel state. He looked around in slight confusion.

"Nice of you to join us!" Aair said.

Gary quickly gained back his bearings.

"What is this place?" he gasped.

The hospital scene was merely a curtain hanging in the fabric of space-time. Around us was darkness, brimming with energy. Dark energy.

Aair answered a moment later, "This is The Void. It is the gateway to every galaxy in the Universe. Be careful! I normally don't travel this way. My travel beacon isn't quite as efficient as a portal, but it's way more interesting and doesn't cause T.A.P.E.! Jopulous is just ahead."

I looked around, trying to find a sign or any sort of clue that had let Aair know that Jopulous was in front of us. There was nothing.

"Aair, how do you know where we are going if you don't travel this way that often?"

He took notice of my concern and smiled, "I forgot you are new to this. You haven't yet absorbed all of the knowledge that The Core has given you. You will know almost everything I know in a few centuries. The Void is not like any other place that you have ever traveled through, sir. You must focus on where you want to go and when you want to arrive. Your thoughts will guide you there. Do not let your thoughts run astray. It can quickly lead to treacherous travel."

I swallowed a lump in my throat.

Aair continued, "I have not been here many times, but I cannot get lost if I maintain focus. You can only walk in one direction in The Void: forward, toward the closest thought. Focus on Jopulous and we will soon arrive."

We walked forward together. I grasped Gary's arm to ensure that he made it through with us. We walked on a floor of darkness that felt like an endless sheet of glass.

"Close your eyes," Aair instructed.

We did as he said and continued forward. My foot splashed into a puddle of liquid. I quickly opened my eyes and looked up.

We had reached Jopulous. We were standing just outside the Dome of the Ardent.

Gary followed us slowly, once again. "That wasn't so ba…"

His sentence was cut short as a Vedren soldier knocked him across the back of the head with a staff.

I gasped and instinctively lunged for the soldier.

Aair grabbed me and held me back. "Relax, sir. He's just trying to help Gary. Trust me, it will be better for everyone."

I relaxed. Aair was much stronger than he appeared.

I sighed and said, "They don't trust him because he's part Leech. I understand that. But, did they have to hit him on the head? Don't they know how bad that is?!"

Aair didn't seem to register my question. He was looking past me, his mouth agape.

I turned around.

What I saw walking toward us is hard to put into words.

A specter approached. It was translucent, but its shape was still visible. In its wake, all matter was consumed by a vortex of darkness, and then replaced further behind as if it had never been affected. It moved toward Gary. We stepped aside, out of the way of the powerful being.

I whispered to Aair, "What is happening?"

He gestured toward the apparition. "It is an ∑œøπåß∂ƒƒ, but there is no pronunciation for that in your language, so you can call it a Myst. There are five in existence, and they communicate only to The Core. It is said that they are so powerful that even the Ardent cannot interfere with their actions. We are merely observers of its work."

The Myst stopped in front of Gary. A deep hum pulsed the air and grew stronger. My eardrums rattled, and my brain felt like eggs being scrambled. The specter raised Gary's unconscious body to his feet.

I saw what happened next in bits and pieces. Tiny moments of clarity revealed an unbelievable scene that I will do my best to describe, although it will be similar to describing a mesmerizing landscape to someone born blind. You cannot fully understand what you cannot perceive.

All surrounding light was extinguished. The scene was only partially lit every few seconds by what looked to be tiny flashes of lightning. Gary's entire body was covered in bright blue flames, but he didn't seem to be burned by them. His body flickered in and out of existence. I was unable to witness the last few minutes of the encounter. It was all that I could do to remain conscious as the waves of energy pulverized my body. I shrank down to my knees and hugged my legs until the passing of the storm.

There didn't seem to be a clear ending to the fierceness of the exchange. I only noticed after some time had passed that the air had become still again, but I hadn't a clue how long the encounter had lasted. I opened my eyes and looked up.

Gary stood upright, facing away from me. His skin was still glowing blue.

"Gary..." I said sheepishly.

He turned to face me. I gasped at the sight of his eyes, entirely black and devoid of all human-like quality.

"I am here," he said, although his words sounded as if two different voices spoke them—underwater.

Aair spoke up, his face filled with astonishment. "I have only heard the tales from the elders, but I did not think that I would witness this in my lifetime."

I stared at him, straining to hold in my nerves.

"What are you talking about? Will you please explain what just happened?"

Aair put his hand on my shoulder and did his best to calm me with an explanation.

"The Mysts are some of the most powerful beings in existence. They are the guardians of Reality. Every few centuries, they deem it necessary to endow another being with their powers for the good of the Multiverse. The Myst has merged with your friend, Gary. He is one of them now, in a sense. I do not know why the Myst has entrusted Gary to carry out his mission, but it seems that we now have a *powerful* weapon against the Leeches."

The entire time he spoke, I couldn't stop staring at Gary.

How much of my friend is still in there? I wondered.

He turned his head in my direction, and—as if he could read my thoughts—he responded, "Do not worry. I am still here. We are very strong now. The Leeches do not stand a chance."

My stomach fluttered with a mix of excitement and fear.

___Z___ Even though I was completely flummoxed at what I had just experienced, I knew it wouldn't get me anywhere to just stand there with my jaw on the ground, so I attempted to act as normal as possible.

"What is our plan, Gary? How will we defeat the Leech army?"

He placed his hand on my shoulder. His skin was cold as ice, but a deep, unexplainable warmth accompanied the cold.

"I shall speak with the Ardent and put together a council for tomorrow morning," Gary explained. "Until then, I want you to go with Aair to the armory. He has a surprise for you."

Aair motioned for me to follow him.

As we walked away, I turned to look at Gary. In shimmering pieces, he began to fade into the horizon, until nothing remained.

AAIR AND I ARRIVED at the armory. The building almost resembled a medieval castle. Flags emblazoned with the Symbol of the Ardent fluttered in the breeze atop the entrance. Two guards stood at the door, and as we approached, they seemed permeated with joy.

"Time Keeper! How are you?" one of them asked.

"I'm alright, I guess," I replied, "considering we are on the brink of war...and my best friend just merged with a magical ghost thing."

The two soldiers burst into laughter as they opened the door to the armory.

"Enjoy your gift!" they shouted in unison.

What the heck is this gift? I wondered.

We walked through a few corridors and into the lab. Here, new proto-types of weapons were being created and tested.

Scanning the massive workshop, something caught my eye. A bright, blue glow peeked out of a wooden crate.

I made my way over, curious about the contents of the container. Peering in, I saw what looked like an axe, except where the handle should have been, there was instead a fuzzy, feathery-looking thing. I reached down to pick up the strange-looking weapon.

Behind me, a familiar voice spoke, "Oh, are you the new maid?"

I turned around. It was Siiva.

I smiled and asked what the strange weapon was.

"That is a feather duster, Jim," she said, holding back a laugh. "Just a little customized, is all."

I dropped the duster in embarrassment.

"Well, what is this gift I keep hearing of, Siiva?" I asked.

She smiled. "Follow me and find out."

We walked to the back of the lab, into a quarantined zone. Siiva un-locked the door and told me and Aair to wait outside.

A few minutes later, the door opened, and Siiva motioned us in. The room was empty, other than a lone table in the center.

Siiva spoke up, "I've been working vigorously on this for about a week, Jimmy. It will help you in the coming fight."

I approached the table.

The gift, no larger than my fist, was wrapped in a black cloth. I uncov-ered the mysterious item. It resembled a smooth, oval-shaped rock. Green light pulsed every few seconds through visible veins in the object.

"What is it?" I asked.

Siiva walked around the table. "I have created a Leech egg, Jimmy. Boral and his Leech army will not harm anyone who possesses this. Leeches value the lives of their young more than anything in their universe, and *you* will have your very own."

A feeling of great relief ran up my spine. Although one thing still puzzled me.

"Siiva, I just talked to you yesterday or earlier today or something... How have you made this egg already? And, aren't you supposed to be at a meeting with the Universal Galactic War Party or something?"

Siiva laughed. "Jimmy. Nearly three weeks have passed here since your short trip on Earth. Remember, the Ardent told you this would happen."

"Well, yeah...I remember that now," I admitted.

"It doesn't matter. You're back and I'm finished with your gift!" she chirped.

I stuttered a little, "I...I don't know how to thank you, Siiva."

She gently placed the egg into my hand. It was warm and had a constant, faint vibration.

"All I want from you, Jim, is to help rid my universe of the Leeches that plague it. Send Boral to the far ends of The Void forever, and restore peace to Jopulous."

A fire ignited inside me.

"I promise you, Siiva, I will do everything that I can to make that happen."

Siiva gave me a warm embrace. "You've come a long way, Jimmy Truffle. I'm proud of you."

I placed 'Lil' Leech' in my bag and exited the armory. Everything seemed to be falling into place. We had all we needed to face the Leeches. I headed to my quarters for some much-needed rest. The war council was meeting early tomorrow morning.

THE NEXT DAY, AN eerie haze hung over the Dome, obscuring the top from view, as if the weather itself knew of the war to come.

I marched inside, determined to devise the ultimate strategy with my new allies. We collected in the council room where a long, glass table stood centered of the Dome with the Symbol of the Ardent etched brilliants into its surface. The Ardent sat at the end of the table in his quaint, wooden chair.

Beside the Ardent stood two guards and General Krael. On the right side of the table sat Appollyon and Warden, the lead strategists, followed by Warrior and Orochi, their fellow combat advisors. The left side seated the people that I knew: Siiva, Aair, and the Mystical Gary.

I took my seat next to Gary and placed the egg on the table in front of me.

The Ardent stood up and slammed his staff into the floor, sealing the doors and windows.

"Let the Council of the Valkyrie begin!"

THE SECRET

7

___C___ SOLEMN FACES AROUND the table stared intently at the great leader. The Ardent took a deep breath and closed his eyes.

"Much time has passed since Jopulous has been at war. I take no delight in matters such as these, but it is my duty, as well as yours, to protect the universe in which we live. We should not think only about our little world here, but the multitude of others that will feel the pain of the Leeches, should we not succeed. I have invited the leaders from every intelligent and allied world in our galaxy to attend this council. They will join us now."

There were fifty chairs bordering the inner walls of the Dome, and as Ardent Holiq finished speaking, great beings began to appear in the chairs. Some arrived sitting normally in the chairs. Some were contained inside strange suits or chambers that sealed them within their required environmental conditions. Some were too big to fit in the chairs, so they stood in front of their seats. One strange creature *became* the chair he was supposed to sit in. The chair now bore an odd-looking face, and it made me a bit nauseous.

In just a few seconds, leaders from other worlds occupied forty-four of the fifty chairs. Each of them gave their sole attention to the Ardent, who resumed his speech.

"The Leeches have long been a growing problem for our worlds. We knew this day would come. It was only a matter of time. Now, we are being forced to deal with it. Such evils will no longer be tolerated. General Krael has been working tirelessly to find a solution that will result in minimal casualties. General, please..."

General Krael rose to his feet.

"It has been only a few weeks since the Leeches began building their army. My intelligence gathers that they are moving faster than we anticipated. Their strength is great, but there is worse news. They possess a weapon that should never have fallen into their hands. They have captured a Myst."

Everyone in the room looked around, astonished. Silence filled the Dome as the General allowed the thought to sink in. The air was heavy with fear and anger, but the faces of the leaders bore no expression of either.

The General resumed. "We do not know how they have managed to capture the Myst or what they intend to do with it, but what we do know is that..."

Gary stood and interrupted, "Sorry to interrupt, General, but the Leech hive-mind tells me that Boral is trying to steal the Myst's powers. They know that the Myst must willingly transfer its power. It will never do that for them, so they are working on a way to destroy the Myst and capture its power."

The room erupted into chatter. General Krael looked insulted by the commotion. The Ardent's staff crashed onto the table and brought order back to the room.

Ardent Holiq voiced his concern. "Gary, I wish you had mentioned this sooner, but I am sure that the Myst inside you knows best. Do the Leeches know how to destroy the Myst?"

Gary shook his head. "Not yet, your Majesty, but even if they find out, they will still have to find a way to capture the power once it is released from the Myst. This will take some time to figure out. I do not believe that the Leeches will invade before Boral has acquired his power. We should strike first, while they are weak."

Ardent Holiq looked to General Krael, who nodded his head in agreement. The Ardent paused for a few moments to silently deliberate, then addressed the room again.

"Gary has given us something new to think about. We must take the time to examine these matters and adjust our strategy. Before we part, does anyone have anything to add?"

Siiva stood and addressed the leaders.

"Your Majesty, I have spent some time researching Leeches and I have used Leech DNA to create a Leech egg. As you are aware, the Leeches will not risk harming one of their own, especially unborn. I have entrusted it to Jimmy Truffle, as he is critical to our mission's success."

General Krael responded, "This is good news. We can put the Time Keeper near our front lines when we attack, and they will be hesitant to harm anyone or anything around their egg. We can use this weakness to get us close to Boral."

The Ardent nodded in agreement.

"Anyone else care to address the council?" he asked.

Seconds passed, and no one spoke up, but after a few moments, a figure stepped forward from the right side of the room. She was a short, green being with an emaciated body and an enormous head.

"Your Majesty, I am Ardent Yrit from Gzunne. I wanted to know if you had received my request."

The Ardent turned his gaze away from the woman and rolled his eyes.

He met her gaze once again and responded. "Ardent Yrit, I understand that your world has found a way to capture and enslave the Leeches, but what we are discussing is a situation that has evolved far beyond such a solution. Your methods of enslavement take time. Time that we do not have. Especially considering the increasingly large number of Leeches. We will keep an open mind, but for now, I believe our chances are better to attack the enemy and not expose ourselves by attempting to capture it. What you are suggesting is very dangerous, and we cannot afford to take unnecessary risks."

The female Ardent looked insulted. *"Please,* your Sovereignty! If we destroy the Leeches, we will be throwing away an opportunity to create a slave-race that will serve our needs in whatever way we please. If we could only..."

Holiq cut her off. "Be silent, Yrit. We have spoken enough today. Let us take our leave and mull over these matters in private."

With that, Ardent Yrit bowed and resumed her seat.

"Dismissed!" Ardent Holiq bellowed as he swung his staff toward the ceiling.

In the blink of an eye, everyone was back on their home planet, and our group was left standing outside the Dome. The heat of the three suns around Jopulous caused a bead of sweat to form on my brow.

Gary grabbed me aggressively by the arm.

"Jimmy, we need to speak in private *this very minute!"*

Gary and I relocated to the Jopulous Gardens.

Nuriignar and another female gardener bug were tending to their strange plants some distance away. Nurii caught our glance and offered a wave. We waved back and watched him dive into the ground, most likely to tend to his extensive and secret underground garden.

We scanned the surroundings for other signs of life. No one else was around. Gary took a seat, and I followed his lead.

"Jim, I didn't want to bring it up in front of the council, but I have a plan."

I stared at him inquisitively. "Go on."

Gary looked around again, seemingly paranoid. "Okay, listen closely. I know this might not all make sense, but you're going to have to trust me."

He paused, as if waiting for a response.

I stammered, "Gary, I trust you! I don't know exactly what's going on right now, but *spit it out* already!"

"Okay, okay," he whisper-shouted. "So, remember when I said during the council that the Leeches have captured a Myst, and that Boral plans to try to steal his powers? I also told Holiq that the Leeches don't know how to destroy the Myst or steal its power. Well, I *may* have lied a little bit..."

I stopped breathing. Then, I screamed, *"Gary,* do you even *realize* what you've done!? The Ardent threatened us with *eternal suffering* if we crossed him. *Whaaaaat* were you thinking!?"

Gary put both hands on my shoulders, but I pushed him away.

"Jim, please listen!" he pleaded. "You *have* to trust me. I won't let this end badly for us. I have a plan and I *know* it will work. Listen. I need to speak with the Core. It is the only thing in the multiverse powerful enough to change the Myst. He can give it the power of a Master Myst, and then we can let Boral steal its powers. Little will Boral know that the Core will have made the Myst *far too powerful* for Boral to handle. He will be overloaded, and his power will destroy him! Trust me. Look, the Myst that merged with me could only give me a fraction of its power because I don't possess the capacity for such power. Boral is a Leech, which I am—in part. I know that Boral can't possibly hold the power of a Master Myst. He will be destroying himself without *any* danger coming to the people of Jopulous *or* our allies."

I processed his words for a moment.

"Gary, are you a *hundred percent sure* that this will work?"

Gary tilted his head up and down—with a slight wobble—and answered, "Let's say 99.9% sure."

I sighed heavily. "Okay. We have to inform the Ardent of your plan. And, you can tell him that you just forgot to mention the rest of the information earlier."

Gary insisted, *"No, Jimmy!* We have to keep this to ourselves. I have a feeling that there is a leak within his ranks, and we can't risk this information getting out."

I blinked rapidly, trying to communicate my doubt to Gary. "Don't you think that Holiq should know if there is a leak in his administration?!"

"No, Jim. If Boral knows that we are planning an attack, he will be forced into stealing the Myst's power sooner rather than later. That's why we need to speak with the Core now! If we move fast and we succeed, no one has to die, except the enemy."

I nodded to show that I understood. Gary grabbed my arm and pulled me into a whirling portal. I saw darkness.

For some reason, I couldn't stop myself from imagining an eternity of suffering.

___**Z**___ I was beginning to get used to the feeling of traveling through space-time. It puts incredible strain on your body. Time and time again, I have heard the audible pops of my joints separating and the grotesque stretching of my flesh as my atomic structure adjusted. I can recognize the sound of my labrum ripping from my scapula as easily as most humans can immediately recognize the sound of their ringtone or alarm clock. It had strangely become quite soothing.

After a few succinct moments of thought, we had arrived at the abysmal center of the Void. For one to meet the Core—Gary explained—they must wait, suspended in the black gulf of nothingness until the Core is ready to present itself.

The quintessential emptiness of the Void—the overwhelming black—can really make a man depressed.

How does the most powerful being in the entire multiverse live in the most boring place? Why not decorate a little? I thought.

Gary responded to my thought. "I always thought that you had no taste in decor, Jim. All those years of cleaning after you made me appreciate simple decoration."

We laughed, reminiscing. So much had happened recently that it seemed like another lifetime ago.

Moments later, the Core began to emerge from the black in front of us. As it neared, I was swarmed with deep thoughts about the Core's existence. Such a powerful entity, crammed into a cloud of something indescribable. It made no sense to me, but I supposed that it didn't have to. It stopped in front of us. A pulse of energy shot through my body, and I immediately hunched over in blissful discomfort.

"It wants to speak with me," Gary said, approaching the Core.

I watched as the interaction began.

Gary cleared his throat, "Certainly you already know, but I am Gary Barnige, part Myst, part Leech, and member of the Jopulous Valkyrie Council. I have come to request your assistance in our conflict with Boral and the Leech army."

The Core rarely communicates with anything, but it responded, directly into Gary's mind, and what follows is their conversation:

Core: *Assistance requested?*

Gary: "Boral, Commander of the Leech army, has a Myst in his possession. He intends to destroy it and absorb its power so that he can defeat us and gain possession of Jimmy Truffle's granradurhatinator. We ask you to grant this Myst with Master Myst powers, so that when Boral destroys it and absorbs the power, he will be destroyed by it. He is a Leech and cannot house such powers in his current form."

Core: *Myst not present. Won't grant power.*

Gary: "You won't give it Master Myst powers because it isn't here?"

Core: *Precisely.*

Gary looked at his hands. Deep beneath his skin, the green fascia would forever be a reminder of the Leech inside him.

Turning towards me, he spoke in a strong, but shaky voice. "Jimmy, travel back to Jopulous and wait for me there. I must speak with the Core alone."

I was puzzled.

"What?! *No!* I'm not leaving you after all we've been through!"

Gary lifted his hand and sent a blinding wave of energy toward me. I lost track of myself for an instant.

I blinked and found myself in the Jopulous Gardens.

Gary, what have you done?

I immediately tried to connect with Gary's thoughts, but couldn't communicate with him. All I received was static.

I MADE MY WAY to the armory, where I knew Siiva would be. She was hard at work on weapons for the upcoming battle, so our conversation was brief.

Helpful as always, she knew right where Gary was. He had just arrived back and was in the Library of Jopulous.

As I walked toward the library, I noticed that—once again—my movements were being watched by a large owl. It appeared to be the same one that I had noticed back on Earth—in the past!

So peculiar!

Clumsily, I tripped over my own feet—ungracefully—again.

After checking to make sure that nobody else saw my fumble, I looked back toward the owl's perch. It had disappeared. I wondered momentarily if it had been a figment of my imagination.

As I continued in the direction of the library, I pondered what Gary's motive was behind speaking to the Core alone, but no obvious answers came to mind. I had to get to the bottom of this, quickly. In approximately nineteen hours, the entire galaxy would be attacking the Leeches.

The library was vast, housing over four hundred trillion books, ranging from Eirnian gardening techniques to Querintinian propulsion manuals. I asked the ancient Vedren librarian if he knew where Gary was. After all, he was now one of the most important people in the city, so I assumed even the librarian would know.

"He went to find books about Mystic powers and phases of destruction. You should find him in aisle M-23,984," the kind librarian informed.

I thanked the gentleman and headed up to the fourteenth floor.

The library had twenty-six floors. One for each letter of the English alphabet. It still amazes me how much Human culture is present outside of Earth—or the solar system, for that matter.

The elevator opened up, and I began making my way to the specified aisle. This floor, unlike all the others, seemed to be empty. A few lights were flickering on and off, which made it a little creepy.

Turning a corner, I saw Gary sitting on the floor with his back pressed up against a bookshelf. He had at least twenty books surrounding him. I walked over and knelt beside him.

"You okay, Gary?" I asked gently.

Gary looked up at me and quickly wiped the concerned expression from his face, as if to hide something.

I pressed again, "Is everything okay? Why did you send me back here? What did you and the Core discuss?"

Gary abruptly stood up and mumbled frantically, "So many questions. So little time."

I placed my hand on his shoulder. "Gary, can you please explain to me what is going on?"

He walked over to one of the study tables and sat down.

I pulled up a chair beside him and awaited an explanation.

Gary scratched his head and let out a deep sigh. "You seem to be very concerned, Jimmy, and you have every right to wonder why I needed to be alone with the Core. You see, as a Myst—even partly so—it is my responsibility to keep all Core business confidential. The Core commanded me to send you away because you are a Hudren. Only Mysts are allowed to have a two-way council with the Core."

He gulped audibly, and I studied his face questioningly.

He continued, "Regarding what we discussed in private, I will share this information with you *only* because you are my dearest friend, and I trust you to keep it confidential. The Core has agreed to transform the Myst into a Master Myst. Our plan to use that against Boral seems to be a sure-fire attainment."

The news wasn't anything unexpected.

"So why do you seem so flustered, Gary?"

He gave me a reassuring smirk. "Oh, you know me! If anything big or significant is about to happen, I get all worked up for no reason."

"Everything will be fine," I said encouragingly. "We've made it this far, right?"

Gary nodded his head. "Yeah. I guess you're right."

I stood up from the table and gave a last remark as I turned to leave.

"Oh, Gary..."

His eyes peeled away from the page.

"We have a briefing tomorrow morning at 0630. The time for war is almost upon us. Make sure to get some rest. Don't stay up too late reading."

He assured me of his light intentions for the night, and I headed off.

I had no idea what troubles haunted Gary, but I hoped for his sake that he would be okay.

THE GREAT BATTLE

8

BEEP. BEEP. BEEP. BEEP.

0600.

The implant in my arm was telling me to get up.

I walked over to my CSC-created mirror. A little self-talk before a big day never hurt.

Okay, Jimmy, ___C___ remember the plan. The egg will keep you safe. Just play along with Krael's battle plan and keep the egg close until Boral inevitably destroys himself. Then we all go home. Simple. The Ardent will understand everything and forgive us once we save the multiverse. I hope.

After a quick bite of my new favorite juilleir fruit, I grabbed my things and stepped outside of my new quarters. I hoped to be sleeping here again tonight. Fingers crossed!

I expected to meet up with Gary on the path as I headed to the Dome. However, I didn't see him anywhere. I assumed that he had just gotten a head start.

I trudged down the narrow path through the Jopulous Gardens, careful to admire all of the plants as I walked by. I knew that our mission would most likely succeed, but I couldn't help but notice a feeling in my gut that this might be my last time walking through this spectacular place.

Relax, Jim. You have the egg. That's your protection. You'll be fine.

Reassured, I hastened my pace toward the Dome.

I arrived at 0622. The mood was somber. All seats from the previous day were filled, including the forty-four around the outer walls.

They must all be thinking about their possible demise, I thought.

I couldn't place myself in their shoes, but I knew I had to act like it.

Gary was already here, looking down like the rest of them—blending in. I realized at that moment that Gary and I were the only two souls in the building who knew of the plan that would guarantee our success. I took a seat next to him. He looked up as I sat and offered a disingenuous half-smile.

Two massive doors at the other end of the Dome opened, and the great leaders approached. The Ardent looked especially normal today. The room stood to show their respect. The leaders took their chairs and ordered the room to do the same. One could have easily heard a pin drop.

Ardent Holiq ended the silence. "In a very short time, the armies of Jopulous and its allies will be facing the armies of the Leeches. It will be the greatest battle that Jopulous has ever seen. The army of Leeches is the largest we have faced. But, we are stronger! They are smart. We are smarter! They have a Myst, and we must hope that they have not figured out what to do with it. We have Jimmy Truffle."

The Ardent's gaze met mine.

"Jimmy possesses a Leech egg, which we are assuming they will try to protect and steal, if they know what's best for them. For us to succeed, every one of you in this room must be willing to sacrifice your life for Jimmy Truffle and his friend, Gary, who has access to the hive mind. They are our only hope in winning this fight. Gary informed us this morning, through intel extracted from the hive mind, that the enemy is already in battle formation. Our plan to surprise attack is no longer viable. However, the foundation of our plan remains intact. We use Jimmy to get close to Boral, and, with Gary's help, we shall destroy the leader of our enemies."

He took a moment in silent thought before continuing.

"Only a few of you have seen the enemy in the flesh. Fewer of you have seen more than one at once. They have strength in numbers. Do not underestimate them! Be strong. Be wise in your strategy. If you do this, we will be *victorious!*"

Everyone stood at the closing of his speech and began stomping their feet in esprit de corps. For several minutes, the energy and volume in the room had me more wired than every cup of coffee I've ever had—combined.

The Ardent took his seat and gave the General a signal. Krael produced a glowing orb from a box in his pocket and held it towards the sky. A beam shot up to the ceiling and bounced back down from a small crystalline globe. Thin streams of green light landed on the heads of everyone in the room; all except the Ardents, who would remain behind to oversee their realms should the armies not succeed.

Using his free hand, the General drew an exquisite sword from its scabbard and thrust it to the sky with a fierce roar. Other voices joined in, unleashing screams from the depths of their souls as they raised their weapons to the ceiling.

The walls of the Dome shook. The sound was deafening. I felt a deep connection to every soul in the room. Regardless of our separate lives in our respective worlds or any of our differences, we were all willing and ready to fight and die for each other in that moment. Our common purpose united our spirits.

The orb in the General's hand began to rise from his open palm toward the ceiling, glowing brighter as it lifted higher. It rose to the pinnacle of the ceiling, and then we were all transported through time and space.

WE STOOD ON A great battlefield—a vast, orange desert with great mountains in the far distance.

About a mile away, the enemy stood in ranks. The frontline of Leeches stretched at least two thousand wide. I turned around to gaze at our army. A hill behind me sloped down so that I could see thousands of troops—armies from the forty-four allied worlds that attended the council. Our numbers were substantial. It was hard to tell from my vantage point if the enemy had more or fewer warriors, but I was sure that either way, it didn't matter. I felt my pocket to make sure the egg was still there.

All good.

Gary grasped my right arm, and I turned to look at him. He was smiling at me. It wasn't a happy smile. It was a smile that could tell a story. A smile that said to me that he was proud to be standing next to me. I returned the smile, and then I crossed my eyes and stuck out my tongue.

His smile turned into a frown.

"This is serious," he said. "We could die today."

"I know," I said. "I'm just trying to lighten the mood."

I checked my side to be sure my weapon came with me. Gary and I wielded swords. Mine was small, so it could be used with one hand, if needed. Gary wielded a hefty broadsword that could cut down multiple enemies with one sweep.

A horn sounded in the distance. The sound was vile. The enemy cheered in a murderous screech. The sound made my stomach turn. A mildly unsettled look came over a few of the faces around me.

In response, General Krael pulled his sword and, once again, thrust it to the sky. He belted out a mighty yell, stronger than the one before. Behind me, a wave of shouts pierced the sky and drowned out any sounds from the enemy lines.

Far off in the distance, in the middle of the Leech army, a giant figure climbed up onto a large rock outcropping.

Boral.

A covered oval cage stood atop the rocky ledge. The giant Leech leader pulled the veil from the cage. A shimmer appeared from inside it.

The Myst.

I looked at Gary. There was a glimmer of fear in his eyes, but he nodded his head. I looked back at the battlefield.

General Krael shouted out again, "Armies of Jopulous. Allies of our world. Protectors of our Universe. Kill them *ALL!*"

With courageous shouts, we broke from our positions to confront the enemy.

We ran.

We ran for a while.

We ran out of breath.

We slowed down.

We wondered why we didn't start out closer.

We got closer.

We found our second wind.

We picked up the pace.

In the moments before the clashing of armies, as the gap closed, time seemed to slow. Senses heightened. Adrenaline churned.

Our army met the Leeches with brute force. Vital liquids spilled in various colors across the battlefield like a violent rainbow. Metal gleamed in the light of the suns, which stood directly overhead.

I cut down any enemy that came near my blade. They seemed mesmerized. The egg appeared to have a trance-like effect on them. They approached me with lowered weapons and outstretched arms. They didn't even seem to notice when I swung my sword. Their attention was fixed on the egg glowing in my pocket.

Gary and I cut a line through the middle of the Leech army, blazing a trail toward the rock outcropping on which Boral stood with the caged Myst.

To my right, General Krael swung his sword down onto one of the larger Leeches, splitting it in two. Yellow ooze seeped out of it, and I stepped onto one half of his body as I pressed forward.

When we were only a few hundred yards from Boral, I noticed that I could make out an expression on his disgusting face. He was laughing.

Suddenly, every Leech turned and faced their leader, who was pulling a dagger from his waist. It shone with a vivid purple glow, undimmed by the daylight. None of the Leeches moved or shifted their gaze from Boral, even as our armies continued to cut them down. I quickly realized why.

The moment has come! He's going to kill the Myst and die!

Just as soon as I thought the words, the leader of the Leeches reached through the cage and plunged the cursed dagger into the powerful Myst. The fight on the battlefield came to a halt as every soul looked up to see Boral siphon the power from the Myst through the dagger.

Boral grew larger by the second until he was three times his former size. His eyes sparked with lightning, and his veins glowed as power flowed through them.

He pulled the dagger from the Myst.

The Myst collapsed, turned to ash, and blew away with the wind.

Boral let out a guttural scream that nearly burst my eardrums. I covered my ears. I looked over to Gary. He was saying something to me.

I couldn't hear it over the scream of the Leech King, but he seemed to be mouthing the words, 'Everything is going to be alright.'

I was confused. Boral seemed to be holding the Myst's power quite well, given his apparent incapacity for Master Myst power. Then it hit me.

It must not have worked. Maybe Boral had enough capacity for Master Myst power after all! Or perhaps the Core had failed to carry out its end of the deal.

Something was wrong. I began to panic. I pulled the Leech egg from my pocket and clutched it to my chest, slightly calming me down.

Boral's gaze immediately shifted to meet mine. He sheathed his dagger and jumped down from his rock. The earth quaked beneath me as he landed. He stalked toward me, pointing his finger in my direction. His round mouth contained many rows of very small dagger-like teeth.

Fear overtook me. I began to look around frantically for a place to run—an escape route.

The egg. He won't risk hurting the egg.

I turned and faced him again.

He was closing in. Fifty meters now.

Thirty.

Twenty.

Ten.

Just before he was within swinging distance of my sword, Gary lunged forward.

Hardly showing any effort, Boral held out his hand, and an invisible force swept Gary backward and pinned him to the ground.

General Krael came from the left, leaping through the air, sword raised.

Boral once again held out his hand, and the General was taken back and pinned twenty feet behind me, near Gary.

Holding up both hands and showing a little more effort, the Leech King forced the entire line of allies and enemies back, until it was just him and me, face to face on the battlefield.

I dropped my sword and held the egg out in front of me.

"Stay back!" I shouted.

Boral laughed in a deep, menacing tone. "You think that you can control me with one of my own? *No one* controls me!"

With a swift motion of his right hand, he yanked the egg from my grasp. He held the egg up above his head. Then, with a cruel smirk, he craned his head upward and dropped the egg into his disgusting mouth.

Leeches throughout his army cried out in sorrow, or pain—it was hard to tell.

I fell to the ground and grabbed my sword. Clutching it with both hands, I shakily held it out in front of me. I stood mortified, staring into the face of my demise.

With little effort, Boral flicked the sword from my hands and set a foot down onto my chest.

"Time Keeper," he bellowed. "We meet again. Not so powerful now, are you?"

He laughed again and pressed his foot down on my chest.

I felt a pain lance through my body. I screamed out in agony.

Boral was just toying with me now.

"Oh, come on, Jimmy. Is that all the fight you have? Probably so, huh? Now, before you die, I need you to tell me where the device you call 'GranGran' is."

I stared up at him with a firm expression.

"Not going to tell me?" he said. "That's alright. I know other ways to get you to talk."

He pointed toward Gary and motioned for him to come closer. An invisible force yanked Gary to my side. The Leech King produced the blade from his side once more and held it to Gary's throat.

"Nooooo!" I screamed.

Boral chuckled loudly. "I knew you had a soft spot for this one."

He used the blade to make a tiny cut on Gary's neck. Blood seeped slowly from the prick.

"Please! Don't..." I yelled out, but Gary interrupted.

"Do it! Kill me, *you stupid Leech.*"

Boral looked back at me with surprise.

"This one has some power in him! He's absorbed a Myst's power, as well. I can feel it. I'll give you one last chance, Jimmy Truffle. Tell me where the device is, or I'll kill your friend and become *even more* powerful."

I wriggled wildly under his foot, trying to get free, but I knew that I couldn't. I gave up, exhausted and panting.

Gary yelled at the beast again, "Boral, I know where the device is. I'll tell you now, and you can do what you want with me, but leave my friend alone! He's done nothing to deserve this."

Boral looked back at me. "Time Keeper, what do you think? Should I listen to him?"

I peered over at Gary, confusion riddling my brain.

Suddenly, I heard Gary's voice in my head. '

Trust me.'

He looked at me, nodded, and then turned to the beast.

"Boral, the device is in Jopulous in the Great Hall that connects to the Dome. We stored it in a secure vault. It should be easy for you to break, and with the entire Army here, there is no one left to protect it. Now, leave us alone!"

Boral let out another echoing laugh. The Leech army joined in.

"Time Keeper, your friend doesn't seem very loyal. Let me show you how Leeches deal with disloyalty."

And when he spoke those words, he plunged the dagger into Gary's skull.

I shrieked out from the furthest reaches of my agonized being.

"*NOOOOOOO!!! GARY!!!!!*"

Power surged in massive waves through Boral's dagger and into his body. Gary's body drained of life. His eyes rolled into the back of his head.

Boral laughed again and seemed to grow larger still and more powerful.

But suddenly, his expression changed. His eyes widened. He looked down.

Gary was laughing this time, which was strangely terrifying to watch, because he still had a dagger in his head.

Boral looked at his arm. Holes of blue light pierced through his flesh.

"This can't be," he yelled out. "What *are* you?!"

Gary let out one last small laugh, and then his eyes rolled back into his head again. He went limp. The Leech King screamed and tore the dagger from Gary's head.

The blue light emanating from his arm crept up his body and reached his eyes. He crumpled to the ground, as if struck by lightning, and turned to a pile of glowing embers.

Wide-eyed and in shock, I crawled over to Gary, whose body lay lifeless on the ground.

I reached out to feel for a pulse.

He turned to ash beneath my fingers.

THE GRIEVING

9

___Z___ THE WIND BEGAN to howl, and all around me, thousands of Leeches crashed to their knees and crumbled into dust, an incredible, but unexpected side-effect of their leader's demise. Their ashes, along with Gary's, were carried away with the wisp of the breeze.

My vision started to blur, and the world around me began to spin. Darkness overcame me.

I AWOKE IN MY room back in Jopulous. A thick bandage was wrapped around my chest. I stood up and peeled it off. My injuries were no longer weighing me down, but my heart was heavier than a ton of bricks. I couldn't believe what had just happened.

Gary had sacrificed himself for me, for us, for the entire universe!

Gazing around my room, I noticed something sitting on the table beside my bed. It was a letter from Ardent Holiq; his seal freshly pressed onto the parchment.

The thoughtful letter began with a sour reminder:

To Jimmy Truffle, *Time Keeper,*

It is with a sorrow deeper than the chasms of Vedros that I deliver this missive. Your dearest companion, Gary—known now throughout the galaxies not merely as a man, but as legend—has fallen. His sacrifice at the climax of the Great Battle stands unparalleled in our chronicles. In the long annals of Jopulous, few have given so fully, so selflessly, so fatefully. The name *Gary* shall not be whispered in mourning, but sung in triumph by the generations to come.

It has been five rotations since the skies burned and the Leech King, Boral, made his final, fatal grasp. My advisors—wise and weary—have spent each waking moment tracing the impossible truth: Gary wielded the power of a Master Myst. How he came upon such a gift, none can say. That he chose not to reveal it to the War Council is... troubling. And yet, one does not scorn the silence of a soul that bore such weight alone.

His death was not in vain. When Boral struck him down, he unknowingly sealed his own doom. The raw surge of Myst power overwhelmed the tyrant, rupturing his form and unmaking every Leech tethered to his dominion. One act. One man. A universe, unshackled.

I send this message not by scribe, but by my own hand, though I am summoned now to post-war councils in Andromara, Lythis Prime, and beyond. Know that, even in my absence, the flame of Jopulous burns brighter than it ever has. The Vedren people, though wounded, rise.

To you, Jimmy Truffle—I say this with all the breath of my authority and the full weight of my gratitude: *You are forever welcome in the gates of Jopulous.* Your deeds, your loyalty, your friendship to Gary... these have not gone unseen. You carry now the Ardent's Blessing.

May the eternal lights shine upon your path,
and may Gary's spirit dance among the stars he died to protect.
—Ardent Serda Holiq
Ruler of Jopulous, Friend of the Fallen

The story was finally clear to me.

When Gary and I met with the Core, he sent me away so he could receive Master Myst powers. Out of the kindness of his heart, he didn't tell me or anyone else of this decision, knowing that his death would surely be the outcome.

A small tear ran down my face. I quickly wiped it away when someone knocked on my door.

I opened the door to the warm face of Siiva. Her eyes were flooded with emotion. She embraced me.

"I don't know what to say, Jim. I'm so sorry. Are you okay?"

I smiled at her. "I am, Siiva. I'm happy for you. For this city. For everyone! But, mostly I'm happy for Gary. He did what he knew was right and went out with a bang. All he ever wanted was to do right by everyone. I'm so proud of him."

She smiled. "I'm proud of you, Jimmy. Are you ready to lay him to rest? The ceremony is in a few hours."

"I think I am. Just give me a moment, if you would," I replied.

She began to head out.

"The procession will be in the center of the Main Garden. Join us when you are ready."

I turned toward the mirror, wondering what to wear. Nothing too bleak. This was a celebration of life, not a mourning of death. Gary wouldn't want it any other way. I decided to wear his favorite suit of mine. The red and black slim-fit always put a smile on his face.

I could hear him in my head, "Oh, sir, you will certainly need me to help fend off all the ladies if you're gonna wear that."

I will miss you, Gary.

I walked outside. The sun warmed my cold skin, and I felt free. Maybe Gary did too.

The Gardens weren't too far away, so I decided to go for a walk. The short trek took me past a few key places: the Library, the Armory, and then Gary's Corner, the new pub built in his honor.

I rambled through the Gardens. They were lush and beautiful as ever, with more exotic plants than pores on my face.

As I neared the center of the Main Garden, I noticed a few rows of chairs filling the space around the Ardent's statue. A stage had been set up with a memorial put together for Gary.

I strolled up to the front row where the familiar faces were. Siiva, Aair, and a few others that I had seen around greeted me kindly. I sat down beside an empty seat. It was reserved for Gary.

The friendly bug-gardener, Nuriignar, climbed the steps to the front of the stage and approached a podium with a rose-like flower that functioned as a microphone. His voice was soothing, a perfect fit for the occasion.

"-reetin-s everyone. I am Nurii-nar, keeper of the Jopulous -ardens. We have -athered here today to honor the passin- of a kind soul and to celebrate his life. He was a friend, and a hero! -ive it up for -ary Barni-e."

Nuriignar's speech impediment made it sound like he said 'Hairy Barney', so the audience was hesitant to applaud initially. However, once the clapping began, it erupted into something incredible.

Nuriignar thanked the crowd. "I'm not usually one for words, or letters for that matter, so I have to invite the man who knew -ary the best to the sta-e, Mr. Jimmy Truffle."

I stood, surprised to suddenly realize that I was being asked to speak...in front of a group. Public speaking wasn't my favorite.

I heard Siiva over my shoulder, "You got this, Jimmy."

When I arrived at the podium, I was overrun with emotion, from deep anguish to genuine felicity. I stared blankly into the rows of onlookers, not knowing which emotion to portray.

Memories flashed through my mind. Clips of the past seemed to play repeatedly in my head of the man who had been at my side for what felt like ages. His face when he first saw my time machine. His drunken nervousness before our first time travel. The cruel, possessed being that burned down the warehouse. The half-Leech sitting in the hospital bed that was beyond ecstatic to see me. The powerful Myst he became. The final smile he left me with.

All of these moments best summed up Gary, my best friend. Even when the world was burning down around him, he always managed to lift our spirits.

My throat briefly opened again, and I gave the crowd a short but heartfelt speech.

"Gary Barnige...was (___C___) a hero. He was a calculated man, but also goofy and loved by anyone who got to know him. He took pleasure in serving the needs of all those around him. His loyalty could hardly be matched." I paused, choking back the tears. "I wish I could have given my life for his, so he didn't have to. I should have died instead."

And with that, I left the podium. It seemed too soon to confront this reality. I needed some time alone.

Siiva grabbed my arm as I left the stage. I turned to face her, my eyes red with tears. She took my hand.

"Jim, if the pain is too great, there are things that we could do to help. We could remove the memory of Gary, and your pain would leave with it."

I pulled away, offended. "*How could you* even suggest that? Regardless of how hard it is to hold onto this memory at the moment, if you take it away, I will *never* know how much his sacrifice meant. I just need to grieve for a little while. I'll be fine in a few days."

Siiva, feeling embarrassed, nodded to show that she understood.

I walked away from the Jopulous Gardens. Unsure of where to go, I closed by eyes and spun around in a circle.

When I stopped spinning, I walked in the direction that I was facing.

I didn't stop walking until the suns began to crest the horizon the next morning.

The morning light broke through the branches of the thick forest around me. I was far from the city. Exhaustion flooded my muscles. I looked around for a place to sit.

A large log covered in shimmering moss sat parallel to a creek that trickled quietly around pebbles smoothed by the slow course of time. Just beneath the surface, the rocks lit up with all imaginable colors. I knelt and cupped my hands in the water to have a drink. It seemed safe enough to drink unfiltered. As I took a seat on the log, I wondered if giardia existed in Jopulous.

A twig broke to my right, across the creek. A strange-looking animal was grazing on even stranger flowers. It reminded me of a deer, but its eyes, ears, and nose were unlike anything I had ever seen. It appeared untroubled by my presence. I wished that Gary were there to see it.

It was around that time that I decided that it was time to talk to the Ardent again. Remembering his absence, I concluded that I would have to speak to General Krael instead.

Jopulous was a dream. It might be nice for retirement, but I missed my home back on Earth. Maybe there I could find some proper closure with Gary's death.

With a newfound resolve, I stood and spun around to head back to the city. I briefly considered instantly transporting myself, but decided to stick to the scenic route in case I never made it back here again.

10

THE RETURN

I ARRIVED BACK IN the city just in time for my stomach to remind me that I hadn't eaten in days. Grief had suppressed my appetite for some time, but now my body was done waiting. I headed to Gary's Corner to grab a bite before speaking to the General.

As I walked into the pub, a few familiar faces nodded in respect upon catching my gaze. I took a seat at a small, round table by myself. The bartender, who goes by WubWub, approached and took my order. There wasn't a lot on the menu that I thought I could stomach, so I went with the seared pterocyrus wings. It paired well with the ranch-like house sauce, but I was afraid to ask the ingredients of that.

WubWub returned just a moment later with a mug of his specialty brew.

"It's on the house, Jim," he said.

I raised my mug in thanks.

Once I finished my meal and my stomach stopped screaming at me, I thanked WubWub and proceeded to the Dome.

Upon my arrival, the guards opened the doors to let me in and paid their respects as I walked by.

The General was seated in his usual position next to the Ardent's empty wooden chair. A thought crossed my mind that they might have the most boring jobs in the universe, but I decided not to share that thought with them. It probably wasn't true anyway. I knelt when I arrived at the base of the stairs that led to the leaders' seats.

"Rise, Time Keeper. How are you managing?" the General spoke softly.

I forced a smile. "I'm hanging in there. But…I've had some time to think about it, and there are a few things that I need to ask."

The General remained motionless, waiting for the first question. His eyes kept my gaze.

"First, General. I would like for everyone to stop calling me 'Time Keeper'. I'm really not sure how that started anyway, and it just brings back painful memories. Just call me Jimmy, or Jim, or anything else, please. Most importantly, though, sir, I am truly honored to be able to remain here in Jopulous, but I feel an aching in my bones to return to my old life on Earth. I don't wish to leave forever, but at least until I'm able to get back on my feet. I need closure. I think that being back on Earth is the only thing that will bring me the closure I really need. I don't want to offend you or your offer to stay, I just need some time. I'm sure I'll be back eventually, to visit, if nothing else."

Krael straightened his posture in his seat and folded his arms across his chest. A smile turned up the left side of his mouth.

"Jimmy Truffle, I believe that you know what is best for you, and it seems that you have thought much on this matter, but you do not have to ask our permission to visit your home. You are welcome to come and go as you please! Siiva has crafted a bracelet that will enable you to travel back and forth whenever you desire."

I breathed a sigh of relief and felt a weight lifted from my chest.

He continued, "My only request is that you do not bring any guests back with you without first notifying us. I trust your judgment. Do take care of yourself, Jimmy Truffle."

I clasped my hands together and bowed to show my appreciation, and I turned to leave the Dome.

"One more thing, Jimmy," the General added.

I turned and said, "Yes?"

"If it eases your mind, being a Time Keeper is something to be proud of. You should wear it as a badge of honor. I believe it will make more sense to you soon enough."

The General stared at something over my head that I could not see.

I turned and left, feeling mildly befuddled.

I SPENT THE REMAINDER of the day walking around Jopulous and bidding farewell to the friends and acquaintances I had met in the short time since my arrival.

Nuriignar seemed especially sad to see me go. He gave me one last bug-hug to gift me roadmaps for Earth, so I wouldn't ever get lost driving again.

What a pal!

Once I had said all my goodbyes, I headed to my quarters to get my things together and return to what my heart knew was home.

On my walk, I was once again confronted by the large, mysterious owl. It was perched on a sign near the edge of the path.

"Okay," I said aloud, looking around. "This is surely not a coincidence! I think you're following me!"

I was stunned to hear the owl reply, not with an audible voice, but rather with a thought injected into my brain.

'Hello, Time Keeper.'

I was temporarily unable to form words, which was surprising given that this was certainly not the strangest thing to happen in the last few days.

The owl's voice once again spoke loudly to my mind.

'You don't even know why they call you that, do you?'

"Call me what?" I replied, bewildered.

'Time Keeper.'

"Who—what are you?"

'I'm a memory, but that doesn't make me less real.'

It leaned forward on its perch, its talons gripping the sign tighter.

'A Time Keeper isn't someone who controls time. That's the mistake most of them make.'

"Then what am I?"

'You're a witness—a carrier. Sometimes, you remember what time forgets. At other times, you hold the echoes of what must never be repeated. But at all times, your role is critical and should not be taken lightly.'

I blinked. "You mean I'm...a historian?"

If owls could smile, then I'm sure I saw one.

'You're a choice made over and over again. A Time Keeper walks into the moment others run from. You don't fix the past. You face it.'

I sighed, taking it all in.

'And when the worlds begin to split, it's your presence that decides what holds and what breaks.'

I swallowed. "Okay. But I'm not ready."

'No Time Keeper ever is.'

The owl spread its wings, ready to leave—but paused.

'You don't have to be perfect, Jimmy. Just present. You're not holding the universe together. Just...holding the line long enough for others to catch up.'

I smiled. For the first time in a long time, it didn't feel like the end of the world—just the middle of a weird, badly-timed chapter.

As the owl vanished into the trees, I waved goodbye and muttered, "Fine. I'll keep time. But I can't be blamed if the universe falls apart! It's not like I got a handbook for this role..."

I began walking back to my room once again.

___Z___ THE NEW BRACELET that I was given had an inscription of Gary's initials on it. Wherever I was, the colors would change according to the current weather.

As I packed up my small bag, the bracelet gleamed blue with pulses of orange in between.

A mirroring of the famous Jopulous sunset, I would imagine.

I took one last glance around my room, remembering when it was just an empty box at the beginning of this journey. Then, I looked at the bracelet and imagined my office, my bed, and my lab back on Earth.

___C___ I shouldered my bag, clicked my heels together, and said, "There's no place like home."

I knew that wasn't how the portal worked, but I had to keep a sense of humor about things.

Following the very brief instructions that Siiva had given me before I left, I pointed my hand in front of me and thought deeply about my destination. The air began to stir in front of me.

Molecules rearranged at light speed, and in mere seconds, I was looking into a blurry, blue-tinged window of my home on Earth.

___Z___ I put half of my arm through the portal. The feeling was incredibly invigorating. I gathered my thoughts and wedged the rest of my body through.

Then, I was home for the first time in what seemed like centuries.

The scent of my wooden desk crept up into my nostrils. I inhaled deeply. *Oh, how I missed that soothing aroma*, I thought.

___C___ For some reason, I was surprised that nothing had changed since we had left the estate.

A sudden sadness crept over me. I hadn't left alone, but I was returning that way.

I pushed the thought out of my mind temporarily. I needed to get settled back in before the flood of emotions took over.

I dropped my bag on the floor, creating an explosion of dust that had accumulated over the time that I was away. ___Z___ Unpleasant hacking followed, as I tried to empty my lungs of the filth.

I headed towards the bathroom to take a much-needed shower.

The water felt different from Jopulous' smooth, untainted water.

After I finished my cleaning, I reached for my towel, which—strangely—was no longer there. ___C___ Even stranger was the fact that the heat was on. It was the middle of July when we first left the estate. It was now late November, and I had not turned on the heat. And, this was certainly *not* a "smart" house. Not yet anyway.

I dried off, dressed, and hunted for the thermostat. Sure enough, the heat had been turned on.

A chill crept up my spine. I had the sudden feeling that I was not alone. ___**Z**___ I turned the heat down to a more comfortable level. I was getting hot and nervous.

Surely, my mind is playing tricks on me... I thought. *This time travel is taking its toll.*

Immediately after turning down the thermostat, I heard the stairs creak. The sound was very distinct, so I grabbed an unplugged lamp from a shelf and headed towards the hallway.

___**C**___ Emulating the mindset of Sherlock Holmes, I quickly ran through several scenarios in my head as I approached the stairs.

Scenario One: There is an animal in the house. Maybe an old pet of Gary's that got loose. *Did Gary have a pet?* I would pin him as a cat person, probably.

Scenario Two: Someone has broken into the house. Possibly a squatter. *That would explain the thermostat—and the missing towel!*

Scenario Three: The sound was just the house settling—*totally normal.* But in my heightened state of awareness, it triggered a spiral of over-analysis and investigative reasoning.

You're getting too deep, Jimmy.

___**Z**___ My hands were so sweaty that I thought I might drop the lamp. The house appeared darker and more ominous than it had just moments ago.

Okay, this Sherlock Holmes thing is getting out of hand.

I made it to the stairs and noticed the handrails had been freshly dusted. I either have a clean-conscious squatter or a ghost of the same breed.

___**C**___ My heart was pounding out of my chest at this point, and just when I thought the suspense couldn't build up any more, the silence was shattered by what sounded like the piercing scream of a young girl.

I have never been so startled in my life! I nearly jumped out of my skin and shrieked a girly scream of my own in response to the terror. I turned to face the sound.

The scream had come from a ghost that looked exactly like Gary, and it looked terrified. I swung my lamp at the apparition, not expecting to hit the horrendous thing at all. But, I knocked the crap out of it and it crumpled to the floor.

I stood over the Gary-like apparition in absolute disbelief and yelled out in a panic, "What on Earth is going on?!?"

The imposter began to squirm on the floor, and I readied my lamp for another blow, but then...it spoke.

___C___ "You've gotta be kidding me. I thought ghosts couldn't hurt you."

I stood confused, staring at it.

We seemed to receive the same thought at the same time.

My eyes widened.

Before I could say it, he blurted out, "Wait, are you real? Is that *you*, Jimmy?"

I was almost too flustered to talk, so I blinked a couple of times to make sure the scene didn't change when I opened my eyes.

"*Gary?!* It's me. But, how are *you* here?! I watched you *die!*"

I had to sit down.

___Z___ I MUST HAVE fainted, because the next thing I remember is waking up on the couch.

Gary stood over me, holding a glass of water.

I sat up abruptly.

Gary grabbed my shoulders.

"Whoooahh! No, sir. Take it easy. You hit your head when you fell."

I looked up at him. A huge knot had formed on his forehead.

"You hit your head, too, Gary."

He belted out a classic Gary chuckle.

"No, sir. This was all *your* doing, you lamp-wielding scoundrel!"

___C___ Over the next few hours, we caught each other up to speed on the events that had transpired since we had been separated by death.

As it turns out, Gary had indeed received Master Myst powers from the Core. Apparently, it hadn't taken much to convince the Core to give him the power. After all, it had to know already how everything would transpire.

I was astonished. Gary had planned so many things to make all this work.

___Z___ But, even after all the explanations, I still had one burning question.

"Gary, how are you here? How are you alive?"

Gary smirked. "Well, you see, once you are a Myst, making a deal with the Core is easier than one might expect. Our deal was that I sacrifice myself in Jopulous for the greater good, and I would be reembodied back here on Earth with full memory of what happened."

I sat back and let out a deep breath.

___C___ After a brief moment of silence, Gary started back up again. "You know, Jim, I'm almost certain the Core has a sense of humor."

I squinted and questioned, "How do you figure?"

Gary replied, "Well, he didn't give me back any of my powers once he sent me back to Earth...except this one!"

He then proceeded to change his arms into green, Leech-like tentacles and wave them around like a wacky, waving, inflatable, arm-flailing tube man.

I burst out laughing.

"It's totally useless!" Gary howled.

Just then, the air around us began to stir.

A familiar sound echoed throughout the room as a blue portal opened to our left.

Aair stepped into the room.

"Nice place you've got here, sir."

I laughed, hardly surprised at this point. "Thanks. What are you doing here, Aair?"

"Well, for starters, I wanted to welcome you back to your home and make sure that you both didn't accidentally kill each other when you met again."

"That nearly happened!" Gary chuckled.

"Wait," I asked. "Did you know that Gary was here—alive?"

Aair raised his eyebrows as he replied, "You know, sir, my position in the galaxy gives me direct and regular access to the Core. It told me all about it! But, don't worry, I won't spill the beans back on Jopulous! You can tell everyone there yourselves."

I sighed. I had been home for less than a day, and I already missed that strange world, so far away from here.

"I hope to get back there someday!" I said.

"I hope so as well, but now that I'm here, I actually need your help..." Aair said, looking back and forth at each of us.

"What is it, Aair?" Gary asked.

Aair looked a bit unsettled as he summed up his issue.

"Well, you see...I was on my way back here, not just to greet you both, but to bring back your GranGran device for you to keep safe here on Earth. But...unfortunately...I was testing a new style of travel—as you know I do—and...I kinda dropped it."

It didn't seem like a huge deal to me.

"Okay. Can you go back to where you dropped it and pick it up?"

A couple of beads of sweat began to appear on Aair's brow. "Well...yes, but I don't know *exactly* where I dropped it."

"But you know the general area where we could find it, right?" I questioned.

"Oh, absolutely! It's somewhere in North America!" Aair stated positively.

"Ha! Well, unless you feel like scouring all of North America, I say we call it a loss! We don't need GranGran anymore anyway!" I said.

A little more sweat beaded up on Aair's forehead. "There is just one issue, sir."

We both looked at him expectantly.

Aair cleared his throat and continued. "We *really need* to find it! If the wrong person manages to pick it up and shorts it out by accident, then everything you have experienced since the last time you traveled through your time machine will be reset."

I thought carefully about the implications of what he was saying.

I would be sent back to the moment when Gary and I first traveled to 1865 together, *as if nothing had happened after that moment.*

In some ways, this didn't seem like such a bad thing to me!

Aair must have known what I was thinking, because he provided valid reasoning to explain why my logic was flawed.

"Sir, think about it this way: You both would be reset back to the moment of your first joint travel over a year ago. Seems fine and dandy *except* for the fact that Gary being reset in this way would void the "terms" of the Core's reinstatement of his body."

He paused to let this sink in, but we were quite grasping it.

He sighed. "Gary would *cease to exist!*"

Now, the full gravity of the news hit me all at once. I collapsed to the floor, breathing fast and shallow.

Gary was holding it together better than I was. He knelt and offered some comforting words.

"Don't worry, Jim. We'll find it! We've faced bigger hurdles than this. Plus, even if someone else finds it, the chances of them getting near it with something titanium are..."

"Not impossible!" I interrupted.

Gary continued. "Jimmy, you invented GranGran. If anyone can find it, surely you can!"

I pulled myself together and stood up, remembering the words from my encounter with the mysterious owl.

"You're right, Gary. We'll find it."

Aair rubbed his hands together. "Let's get busy!"

\<END\>

TO Learn more:

IF YOU'D LIKE TO learn more about the two authors—Cory and Zachary Barber—their creative process, and everything they have to offer (including books, future projects, merch, and more), head over to **wormholebros.com**.

Stay in the loop with everything happening inside the Wormhole by subscribing to the newsletter. Sent out frequently, it offers much more than what's on the website—like access to the **Bonus Content Vault**, where you'll find deep dives into backstories, character interviews, exclusive short stories, and more.

Join the growing crew here: **wormholebros.com/newsletter/**

This page is intentionally blank (well...not anymore), because the printer required an even page count. To make it worth it for the tree that gave it's life for this page, you could draw a picture on it, jot down some notes, or just save the space for autographs at a future author signing event ;)